She heard the slam of the Rolls's door

Joanna's thoughts came agonizingly back to the present as she realized that Joshua was home. She had lost hours reliving the time they had met and she had fallen in love.

He didn't say the usual curt good-night at the door, and Joanna stiffened as Joshua came in to sit on the side of her bed. His eyes took on the look of a storm-tossed sea, his breathing suddenly ragged.

He groaned low in his throat, "God, Joanna, I—" and her suspicions were confirmed.

She recoiled even as his hands tightened on her arms. "No!" she gasped, looking up at him with wild eyes. "I don't want to!"

"But *I* do, Joanna," he bit out grimly. "Tonight it has to be yes!"

His mouth claimed hers, parting her lips as he bent her to his will, kissing her with an intimacy she'd thought forgotten.

Books by Carole Mortimer

HARLEQUIN PRESENTS

These books may be available at your local bookseller.

For a free catalog listing all titles currently available, send your name and address to:

Harlequin Reader Service
P.O. Box 52040, Phoenix, AZ 85072-2040
Canadian address: Stratford, Ontario N5A 6W2

CAROLE MORTIMER

the failed marriage

𝓗𝓪𝓻𝓵𝓮𝓺𝓾𝓲𝓷 𝓑𝓸𝓸𝓴𝓼

TORONTO • NEW YORK • LONDON
AMSTERDAM • PARIS • SYDNEY • HAMBURG
STOCKHOLM • ATHENS • TOKYO • MILAN

For
John and Matthew

Harlequin Presents first edition March 1984
ISBN 0-373-10675-0

Original hardcover edition published in 1983
by Mills & Boon Limited

CHAPTER ONE

'WE'RE really interested in running a series of these books,' the man sitting across the desk from Joanna told her. 'If you can write others as good as this first one.'

Joanna shrugged. 'I'm not sure that I can.'

The man's smile of confidence seemed to say he was used to dealing with temperamental authors—and that he was usually the victor. He was a man of middle age, his kindly exterior belied by the sharpness of his icy blue eyes, a sense of purpose about him that told the young woman seated across the desk from him that he could be a very shrewd businessman.

Joanna had never been to a publishers before, and the image of a sterilely white and chrome-painted office, modern in the extreme, had given way to a cluttered room that looked more like a lawyer's office, with manuscripts and books littering the desk-top.

She had guessed when she received the written summons to see James Colnbrook that there had been a favourable reaction to the children's book she had submitted to him several months ago about a playful boxer dog called Billy. But a series of books could be quite out of the question.

'I'm not sure I have the time to write any more,' she told him smoothly. 'It's taken me months just to sit down and write this one.'

'And sometimes it takes years, even when you have all the time in the world,' he dismissed easily, obviously not taking her objections seriously. 'But I'm sure you can do it, Miss Radcliffe,' he encouraged softly.

She met his gaze with steady blue eyes, a coldness coming over her. 'Mrs,' she corrected abruptly. 'Mrs Radcliffe.'

She could see James Colnbrook mentally reassessing the situation, knew that with her cap of blonde curls, gaminly attractive face, and small slender body, she didn't look old enough to be married, not even the obviously expensive clothes she wore, the black silk blouse and fitted black skirt adding the maturity expected of a married woman. But she was married, very much so. At twenty-three years of age she was locked in a marriage that meant nothing to her, as she felt sure it meant nothing to her husband.

'I'm sorry, I didn't realise.' James Colnbrook was smiling once again, having correctly assessed the expensive engagement ring and diamond-studded wedding band he had just noticed for the first time on the slender finger as having cost a small fortune.

Joanna shrugged. 'It isn't important, is it?'

'No. No, of course not,' he dismissed lightly, noticing more and more about her as the meeting progressed. When Joanna Radcliffe had walked into his office half an hour ago he had placed her as a career woman, someone with the style and elegance of an executive secretary, possibly an executive herself. Now he noticed the vulnerability that hadn't been there until her marriage was mentioned, the cool detachment in steady blue eyes, the almost wistful twist to her mouth, her body so thin she looked almost boyish. And lastly he noticed the pain etched into a face too young and beautiful to have known the agony that had put the fine lines beside her nose and mouth. Joanna Radcliffe was a woman who had known deep misery in her young life, and while she seemed to have survived it, it had not been unscathed. 'Does your husband mind the idea of your working?' James Colnbrook gave a forced laugh, feeling compassion for a woman he barely knew, and as his reputation as one of the toughest bastards in publishing hadn't been undeserved it was a strange and alien emotion for him. It made him feel uncomfortable. 'Some men have their macho image to protect,' he mocked.

She seemed to stiffen. 'Joshua has no reason to worry about his macho image,' came the cool reply. 'It's perfectly intact.'

Joshua Radcliffe—the name meant something to him. And yet he was sure he didn't know the man personally. 'So he won't mind if you spend several hours a day working?' he spoke absently, still puzzling over where he had heard the name Joshua Radcliffe before. And it had been lately too.

'When I said I may not have the time to write further books I didn't mean my husband would object,' this time her voice was even icier, 'I simply meant *I* wouldn't have the time. I don't really see what my husband has to do with any of this, Mr Colnbrook. Either you want to publish the book or you don't, regardless of whether or not there'll be others.'

'Oh, we do,' he said swiftly, then cursed himself for revealing too much. The mad escapades of a lunatic dog made a good book, and it would probably sell well, but he had to admit that Joanna Radcliffe intrigued him more—more than any other woman he had ever met.

She was obviously a young woman of breeding, her coolly detached tones acquired through private schooling, the casual clothes she wore most probably having the same designer label his wife's did. Only they would never look this good on Moira! Joanna Radcliffe wasn't the usual type of female author he had in his office, he realised that now. She looked as if she should be spending her time at tea-parties and socially select events, arranging charities, idling the hours away while her husband went out and earned the money, even the mention of the word a vulgarity to her. But Joanna Radcliffe gave the impression of being a very self-possessed young lady, of having only contempt for such useless activities. James's curiosity about her grew by the minute.

'Yes, we would like to publish the book, Mrs Radcliffe,' he was cool himself now. 'But we do like to know a little about our authors.'

'Why?'

'Why?' He was beginning to wonder which one was the publisher and which the budding author! 'We usually like to put a little section about the author on the back of our books,' he explained.

She had begun shaking her head before he had even finished. 'I don't want that,' she informd him haughtily. 'And the book will not be published under my real name.'

'Not under—Why?' he frowned his surprise. Most people longed to have their name on the front of a book, although not everyone was blessed with a name as acceptable as this woman's, as he had once had to explain to one Agnes Snotty!

Cool blue eyes looked at him steadily. 'I would just prefer it that way.'

'But——' he stopped as he saw the light of determination in her eyes. 'Okay,' he sighed, 'I'm sure we can come up with something else you like, but I——' Joshua Radcliffe! Of course, it had come to him now.

He looked at the woman sitting opposite him with new eyes. Surely this young woman couldn't be married to *that* Joshua Radcliffe? The man was a Harley Street specialist, an expensive one at that—and he should know, he had paid the bill for Moira's operation not too long ago! But the man must be years older than Joanna Radcliffe. Not that James had ever met the man, Moira having dealt with all the details herself, he being one of those people who couldn't stand doctors or anything to do with them. He had been given hell by his wife because he had only been able to force himself to visit her at the clinic twice in all the time she was there.

But the mere fact that the man was in Harley Street meant he had to be in his thirties or forties at least. Maybe the man had a son with the same name that this woman was married to?

Joanna was aware of none of James Colbrook's curiosity about her, glancing at the gold watch on her slender wrist, picking up her clutch bag, her nails painted the same deep red as her lip-gloss. 'I'm afraid I have a luncheon appointment,' she told him smoothly. 'I have to go.'

'Oh, but I usually take new authors out for lunch——'

'I'm sorry,' she stood up, the high heels on her black sandals adding to her diminutive height, 'but I do have to go. I wouldn't want to be late for my appointment.'

James Colnbrook stood up too, a look of exasperation on his still handsome face. Tall and dark, with an air of distinction he obviously cultivated, he wasn't a man accustomed to being dismissed by women, especially women as beautiful as Joanna Radcliffe.

But Joanna knew enough of tall distinguished men not to be impressed. After all, she was married to one.

'When am I going to see you again?' James demanded.

'Perhaps your secretary could call me,' she dismissed, already at the door.

'But——'

'I've enjoyed meeting you, Mr Colnbrook. And I'll give the idea of writing more books some thought. Goodbye.' She left with her head held high, not seeing James Colnbrook sink dazedly back into his chair, shaking his head in bewilderment.

Joanna nodded coolly to the secretary on the way out, easily stopping a passing taxi once she was outside to take her to the restaurant where she was lunching with her mother. No one looking at her could have guessed at the thoughts going through her beautiful head.

She was going to have a book published! She, Joanna Proctor Radcliffe, had written a children's book good enough to be published! After years of feeling as if she were no more than Joshua's wife, she was at last able to claim she had done something without his help or influence. Not that there would be much money in her writing, James Colnbrook had already warned her, but just to have some sort of independence, if only an intellectual one, was something to her. And she didn't need the money; she was married to a rich man, was rich in her own right from a legacy left to her by her grandmother several years ago. No, this feeling of accomplishment was what she needed, what she *craved*.

Her mother was already seated at their table when Joanna hurried into the restaurant, several minutes late despite her hasty departure from the publisher's office. And her mother made no secret of her dislike of unpunctuality; just her look of disapproval was enough to dispel some of Joanna's inner elation.

'Sorry I'm late, Mother.' She glided into the seat opposite the other woman, accepting with a smile the sherry the waiter placed in front of her, her preferences being well known in this particular restaurant.

'That's all right, Joanna.' Her mother's voice was sharp; she was an older version of Joanna, her hair kept the same glowing blonde as her daughter's by a gifted hairdresser she frequented, her face and body still beautiful in her forty-fifth year.

Joanna flushed at the lack of sincerity in her mother's voice, feeling, as she always did in her presence, like the gauche schoolgirl she had once been and not a woman who had been married for five years. 'I was delayed at the publishers'.' She sipped the sherry, dry, just as she liked it.

The two women made a startling pair as they sat together, looking more like sisters than mother and daughter. Cora did everything cosmetically possible to maintain her youth, while Joanna had a maturity beyond her years.

'What did he say?' Her mother's query was made out of politeness. Joanna refused to show any hurt caused by her mother's obvious lack of interest, not expecting any gold medals from anyone in her family for anything she did. Her father was a prominent banker, her mother his accomplished hostess, and Joshua—well, Joshua was a success at whatever he did. Her minor achievement would be unimportant to them all. Only she would know of the new inner pride in herself.

She shrugged coolly, accepting the menu placed in front of her. 'They're going to publish it.'

'Really?' her mother's eyes widened. 'It's about a collie or something, isn't it?' she said vaguely.

'A boxer,' Joanna corrected flatly, wondering why she tortured herself with these weekly luncheons with her mother. She always ended up being hurt by her mother's indifference to anything that happened in her life; it would have been more sensible just to have gone to the monthly Sunday visits with Joshua the only time she ever saw her father. Both her parents lived such hectic lives that they didn't really have the time for her. They never had done; she had accepted that very early in her life. Her marriage to Joshua had been her one redeeming feature as far as they were concerned, although in the beginning even that had been heralded as a disaster. 'Like Billy,' she added softly.

'Really, Joanna,' her mother snapped. 'The dog has been dead for years!'

'Maybe. But I loved him.' When she was a child her father had impulsively bought her a boxer. He had forgotten her birthday one year, and had seen the puppy in a pet-shop window on his way home, going in to buy it without considering the fact that his wife might not approve. Joanna had loved the puppy from the first, and despite shrill protests from her mother had somehow persuaded her father to let her keep him. Billy had chewed any and everything in sight, from the furniture to her mother's shoes, and it was after finding half a dozen expensive pairs of the latter chewed beyond repair that Billy had been banished to the garden and kitchen only. Not that he seemed to mind, enjoying chasing butterflies in the summer, and falling asleep in the warmth of the kitchen in the winter. And Joanna had made no complaints either, just being relieved to be able to keep the dog.

Billy had been her constant companion for nine years, until a mad excited dash into the road after a car had caused his sudden death. She had never forgotten him, or the unselfish love he gave her, and the character of Billy Boxer was based on him and the endearing— and often mischievous—things he did.

Her mother gave her order for lunch, waiting while Joanna did the same before speaking again. 'You mean a publisher is actually willing to pay you money to write about a pest of a dog?' she derided in her haughty voice.

'Yes,' Joanna bit out resentfully.

'I don't know what the world is coming to,' Cora shook her head. 'What does Joshua think of all this?'

Joanna's mouth firmed angrily, and she looked nothing like the composed young woman who had left James Colnbrook's office half an hour earlier. 'He hasn't said a lot about it,' she mumbled.

'I should think not! A man of his reputation and standing having a wife who writes children's stories!'

Joanna stiffened. 'I didn't say he disapproved of it, Mother, we just haven't discussed it very much.' They didn't discuss anything any more, they were barely civil to each other!

Her mother opened her mouth to say something, then stopped as the waiter began to serve their meal, the avocado pear deliciously ripe, the prawns nestling in its well pink and juicy.

'You were saying, Mother?' she prompted after the first mouthwatering spoonful.

She received an irritated look. 'Not while we're eating, Joanna. We'll talk later.'

Joanna ate her meal with unhurried grace, her wrists small and delicate, her hands long and slender, seeming weighed down by the rings on her wedding finger.

The coffee stage of their meal came round soon enough, and she prepared herself for more lectures on the inadvisability of having a career when her husband was such an important man, when he needed a wife to perform all the social graces for him. She had heard it all before, in fact she had become sick of hearing it over the years. *Billy Boxer* might not be everyone's idea of a great achievement, but it was the one thing she could truly call her own, the one thing that didn't belong to Joshua or that he hadn't given her.

'. . . and so I was just wondering how he is.'

She blinked, her mother's beautiful face and the sound of the other people talking in the restaurant fading back into her consciousness again. 'How who is?' she frowned.

'Joshua, of course. I realise you're excited about your book, Joanna, but do listen! Your father and I missed Joshua at lunch last Sunday, I wondered how he is.'

Joanna shrugged. 'I told you, he had to go back to the clinic last Sunday. He sent his apologies.'

Her mother frowned. 'He seems to be—working rather a lot lately.'

'Joshua has always worked hard, you know that.'

'But he seems to be working extra hard the last few months.'

Joanna looked at her mother's expectant expression, sighing deeply. 'If you have something to say, Mother, then say it. I don't feel like playing games.'

Her mother looked irritated. 'Are you happy with Joshua, Joanna?'

She looked away. 'Of course.'

'I know that at first your father and I didn't approve of your marriage——'

'Approve?' Joanna echoed scathingly. 'As I remember, you objected very strongly—until you knew exactly who he was.'

'That isn't true!' her mother protested indignantly. 'I never doubted that Joshua was *somebody*. He's just so much older than you. None of us were sure you were mature enough for marriage, but in the circumstances . . .'

'Just tell me what you have to say, Mother,' Joanna interrupted tautly, knowing her mother too well to be deceived by this show of concern for her welfare.

'Well, I've heard——'

'Yes?' she prompted tensely as her mother hesitated.

'It may only be gossip——'

'Mother!'

'There's talk that Joshua may not be spending all his time away from home working! There, I've said it now.' Cora sounded quite shaken. 'I feel so much better now that I've just said it. And it could only be talk—you know how Jackie Simms loves to gossip. I don't——'

Joanna had stopped listening, lost in her own thoughts once again. Her mother might feel better for having dropped this bombshell, but it certainly didn't have the same effect on her. She and Joshua had had their problems over the years, but she had never in all the time of their marriage suspected there could be another woman in his life. Of course Joshua was a sensual man, and she——

'—and I've always told you that Angela Hailey is too pretty to be a mere secretary and receptionist to any man, let alone one as attractive as Joshua,' her mother continued.

'Angela Hailey?' That part of her mother's conversation pierced her tortuous thoughts. 'Are you saying she's the woman involved?' she frowned.

'According to Jackie,' her mother nodded. 'Of course she can't always be right, but she usually is,' she added petulantly. 'And Angela is a lovely woman.'

A mental picture of the beautiful redhead came to mind, her eyes a deep flashing green, her figure shown to advantage in the styled clothes she always wore, her hair long and straight to her shoulders. She had been Joshua's receptionist and secretary for the last seven years now, and Joanna had met her lots of times—and their dislike was mutual. Angela made no attempt to hide her contempt of Joanna whenever they were alone, although she was always coolly polite in front of Joshua. Joanna had always felt it wiser to ignore the other woman's antagonism, but this had only seemed to anger her more. Yes, she could see Angela Hailey as Joshua's mistress, knowing the other woman would revel in such a role. And Joshua had a weakness for redheads—hadn't he been with one when she had first seen him?

She shrugged now. 'There's always talk about a man like Joshua. Half of his women patients would like to claim an affair with him, and the other half want to mother him. If I listened to, or believed, half the gossip of affairs between Joshua and other women I'd be a nervous wreck!'

Once again her mother looked irritated. 'And no one could ever accuse you of having bad nerves, could they, Joanna?' she snapped. 'You're so cool it's unbelievable. Joshua could be having a roaring affair with Angela Hailey and you would simply sit back and deny it!'

Joanna met her mother's exasperated gaze with steady blue eyes. 'Would you rather I said it was true?'

'If it is, yes!'

She sighed. 'I think Joshua is the one you should be asking, not me. Don't they say the wife is always the last to know?' she added dryly.

'Don't you care?' her mother snapped.

'Of course I care,' she bit out, her eyes flashing. 'Joshua is my husband. But he isn't likely to tell me whether or not he's having an affair with Angela, even if I were to ask him—which I'm not going to do,' she added firmly.

'You trust him that much?'

No, she cared that little! If there was another woman in Joshua's life, even if it was Angela Hailey, then she didn't care! 'We're married,' she said flatly. 'I have no reason to think that will ever change. If it does,' her voice was brittle now, 'you can be sure I'll let you be the first to know, so that you can tell Jackie Simms some first-hand gossip for a change!'

'Joanna, don't be flippant——'

'How am I supposed to act?' she rasped. 'You've just told me the biggest gossip in town believes that my husband is being unfaithful to me. Should I shout and scream? Would that make you happy?'

Her mother looked about them selfconsciously as Joanna's voice rose over the last. 'I'm thinking of *your* happiness,' her tone was low. 'That's why I've told you about Joshua. Lots of men—stray. Why, even your father—But that's another story,' she hastily dismissed at Joanna's sudden look of interest. 'But if you know what's going on then you have a chance to stop it.'

Did she want to? Did it really bother her that much any more what Joshua did? She knew the answer to that only too well. And her mother would be deeply dismayed if she knew of her real feelings for Joshua.

'I have to go, Mother.' She picked up the bill. 'I believe it's my turn,' she said lightly. 'I'll see you next week as usual,' and she stood up.

'Joanna——'

'Yes?' She looked down at her mother, seeming much older than her twenty-three years.

'Just—Remember what I've told you!' Cora looked worried by Joanna's attitude. 'Joshua is a man of— experience, sophistication.' She frowned. 'Don't blame him too much if this does turn out to be true. I'm sure it's nothing more than a fleeting affair. Oh, and congratulations on the book,' she added absently.

'Thank you, Mother,' Joanna said dryly, knowing how much of an afterthought the good wishes had been.

She took another taxi home, to the house she shared with Joshua in Belgravia, although perhaps shared was too intimate a description; they both just happened to eat and sleep there, they hadn't shared anything worthwhile in a long time.

The elegant house had been run very efficiently by Joshua's housekeeper before they were married, and Mrs Barnaby continued to do so now, her presence unobtrusive and very ordered, never a jar or hiccup in the routine of the household. Breakfast was always at eight o'clock, lunch always at one, and dinner always at seven-thirty sharp. The house was always spotlessly clean, everything at Joanna's fingertips day and night— and she hated it, from the brass handles on the doors to the crystal chandelier in the lounge. It wasn't a home, it was a hotel, a very beautiful hotel, but no less impersonal.

She nodded coolly to the maid as she opened the door for her, glancing idly at the mail that had been left on the hall table, the heady scent of the carnations in the vase there pleasant to the senses. Most of the letters were for Joshua, as usual, but there was just one letter for her, an invitation to dinner from one of Joshua's medical colleagues. She left this with the other mail, knowing it would be Joshua's decision whether or not they went. They probably would.

'Any messages, Mrs Barnaby?' she asked the housekeeper as she came through from the kitchen with a pot of tea.

'Just from Mr Radcliffe,' the woman informed her without emotion, her rigid nature reflected in her appearance, from the tight bun of hair at her nape to her no-nonsense shoes. 'He said to tell you he'd be home for dinner at seven as usual.'

'Thank you,' Joanna nodded, pouring herself a cup

of the tea. 'I'll take this upstairs with me,' she nodded dismissal, ignoring the other woman's look of disapproval. She had become impervious to those looks over the years, knowing the housekeeper didn't approve of drinks being taken upstairs.

Her bedroom was evidence of Joanna's own self-indulgence, a beautiful boudoir in white and pink lace, even the four-poster bed having white lace curtains that could be drawn at night. As a child she had always dreamt of a room like this, and while her parents had always given her everything money could buy, they had considered such a room ridiculous. When they were first married Joshua had been inclined to satisfy this whim of hers, but had insisted that the adjoining bathroom and his own bedroom on the other side of this remain free of feminine frills.

Separate bedrooms. Joanna had hardly been able to believe it when they were first married, but Joshua's claim about not disturbing her if by some unlikely occurrence he should happen to be called out to the clinic during the night had seemed a valid one. Now she was glad they didn't share a room; she couldn't have borne to share a bed with him all night, every night.

Her mother's suggestion of an affair between Joshua and his receptionist/secretary at the fashionable consultancy he ran in Harley Street didn't seem so unlikely when she considered the amount of time he spent there, an image of the ultra-elegant consulting-room and lounge coming to mind as a scene for the affair. No, it didn't seem so impossible, but Joanna deplored Joshua's choice of mistress, knew that any number of women would have been willing to have an affair with him.

She heard the quiet throb of the white Rolls-Royce at the front of the house at exactly seven o'clock, checking her appearance in the full-length mirror as she heard the deep sound of Joshua's voice as he greeted the housekeeper downstairs. There would have been a time when she herself would have run down the stairs to greet him, but those days were long gone.

They always dressed for dinner, and she had chosen to wear a black gown caught across one shoulder, leaving the other shoulder and arm bare, a gold slave bracelet pushed up on to the completely bare arm. The gown moulded to the slender curves of her body, once again high-heeled sandals adding to her diminutive height. Her make-up was perfect, her hair loose blonde curls that clung to her head, her expression coolly composed as she went down to the lounge to wait for Joshua to join her.

She was sipping her sherry when he came into the lounge fifteen minutes later, his hair still damp from the shower he had just taken. Joanna was able to look at him objectively, to see how the black evening suit fitted the broadness of his shoulders, the trousers tailored to the lean length of his legs.

At thirty-seven Joshua was still probably the most handsome man she had ever seen, his hair dark and thick, tinged with grey at the temples, his eyes a deep piercing grey, his nose long and straight, his mouth a thin uncompromising line, the firmness of the jaw telling of the authority that came as a second nature to him.

The grey eyes were hooded now, almost expressionless as he looked down at her. 'Congratulations.' His voice was low and controlled, almost as expressionless as his eyes.

Looking at him now Joanna could see that he too had changed since their marriage five years ago, that there was hardly a trace left of the man she had first met and been instantly attracted to. Deep lines of cynicism were now grooved beside his mouth, and she could see the years hadn't dealt kindly with him. Could it be that Joshua was as dissatisfied with their marriage as she was? His affair with Angela seemed to say he was.

'Your mother telephoned me,' he explained at her silence, moving to sit in the chair across from her. 'She told me about the book. You must be very proud.' He sipped his whisky.

'Yes,' she nodded.

The grey eyes narrowed, fine lines fanning out from their corners. 'She also seemed concerned about you.'

Her shoulders stiffened at her mother's underhand method of interfering. 'I can't imagine why,' she dismissed coldly.

'You are looking pale——'

'That's because I'm hungry!' She stood up, determinedly putting an end to the conversation. 'Shall we go through to dinner?'

'Of course,' he nodded abruptly, and stood up too, at least a foot taller than she was.

In that moment Joanna wondered where all the charm and laughter had gone from his handsome face, noticing that his muscled body was leaner too, that his cheeks were almost hollow beneath the healthy tan, his long hands still strong and dependable, although they too looked leaner. Yes, Joshua was far from happy in this marriage too.

Their conversation was slow and impersonal through dinner, as it usually was, Joshua asking her a little about the book; but her abrupt replies were not encouraging. Joshua refused wine with his meal and also a brandy afterwards, and Joanna knew what that meant.

'I have to go back to the clinic for a few hours,' he told her as he replaced his empty coffee cup on the tray.

'Yes.' She had known what was coming.

He seemed to hesitate. 'What will you do?'

'Have an early night. Read a book.' She shrugged. 'Don't worry about me, I have plenty to do.'

He was frowning darkly. 'But I do worry about you, Joanna. You must get very lonely here on your own in the evenings when I go back to work . . .?'

'No,' she told him coolly. 'I find ways of occupying my time.'

'I'll go and change, then.' He turned abruptly, going up to his bedroom.

Joanna dismissed the housekeeper for the night once she had come in to remove the coffee tray, and went slowly up to her own room. She could hear Joshua in the adjoining bathroom, and suddenly the idea of a long soak beneath scented bubbles seemed very appealing. She undressed to don her silk robe, sitting down in front of the dressing-table to cleanse off her make-up.

She heard Joshua leave the bathroom a few minutes later and so she went through herself. Everything had been left as neat and tidy as usual, not even the toothpaste tube out of place, squeezed meticulously from the bottom.

She ran the water into the deep sunken bath before searching through the bathroom cabinet. The wide cuff of her robe caught the top of a medicine bottle, unbalancing it, and Joanna watched as it fell, almost in slow motion it seemed, to shatter on the floor.

The adjoining bathroom door was instantly flung open, and Joshua took in the situation at a glance. He was dressed for work now in one of his superbly tailored three-piece suits, grey tonight, with a white silk shirt. 'Don't move,' he instructed tautly.

But his warning came too late. His unwarranted presence here when she was dressed in only a robe caused an involuntary reaction in her, and she stepped backwards, straight on to the glass, gasping her pain as a piece pierced the sole of her foot.

'Stand still!' Joshua rasped as she would have moved once again, crunching across the glass in his shoes to swing her up into his arms and carry her through to her bedroom.

Joanna froze at his physical contact with him, lying stiffly in his arms, beginning to breathe again only when he had placed her on the bed and moved down to examine her foot. If he were aware of her aversion to his touch he gave no sign of it, treating her as impersonally as he would any other patient.

'It doesn't look too bad,' he straightened. 'I'll just get something to clean it.' He went back into the bathroom, turning off the bath-taps as he did so.

Joanna took this few moments to collect her thoughts together, to try and gauge her reaction to being touched by Joshua after all this time. She didn't have one, not revulsion, and certainly not excitement. It had been as if she were being touched by a stranger, and not the man she had shared her most intimate moments with, not the man she had once loved so much. Where had all that love gone?—because it certainly had gone!

She could look at Joshua now and see all the things she hadn't seen in the beginning, the coldness in his eyes, the lack of emotion in his handsome face, the flashes of hardness she often felt in his actions. Yes, she could see it all now, now that it was five years too late.

He was back in her bedroom now, bending over her foot. 'Sorry,' he murmured at her gasp, the jagged-looking piece of glass now in his hand, a wad of gauze stopping the flow of blood. 'Does it hurt?' he asked softly as he bandaged the foot after cleaning it.

'Not too badly,' she shrugged off the digging pain she could still feel. 'Aren't I lucky my husband is a doctor? she added lightly.

Joshua looked up with a heavy frown, searching her face for signs of the sarcasm evident in her voice. 'Yes,' he answered abruptly, his mouth tight, finishing off the bandage before straightening. 'That should be all right now, but the bath is out, I'm afraid.'

'It's only a question of keeping my foot out of the water—isn't it?' she said sharply.

He shrugged. 'Yes.'

'Then I'll still have my bath—thank you.'

His mouth twisted. 'Go ahead. I'll just go and clean up the mess in the——'

'I'll do it.' Joanna flushed, and swung her legs to the floor, pulling her robe hurriedly together as it parted slightly to reveal her nakedness.

Joshua turned away uninterestedly. 'Please let me do it,' he said hardly. 'I wouldn't like there to be any more accidents.'

Her eyes flashed her resentment of his patronising tone. 'Do it, then,' she dismissed curtly.

With a coldly assessing glance in her direction he went into the bathroom, leaving Joanna seething. Anyone would think she had knocked the damned bottle over on purpose!

'All done.' He was back within minutes. 'What were you doing in that side of the cabinet anyway?' he asked mildly.

'Looking for something,' she mumbled, unable to meet his gaze. They each had their own side of the spacious bathroom cabinet, and she was as aware as he that she had knocked the bottle from his side.

Joshua didn't move, dominating the room with his height and breadth. 'What?'

'Just something,' she snapped. 'Look, I couldn't find what I was looking for in my side, so I wondered if Mrs Barnaby had put it back in your side this morning when she tidied up,' she defended as he still seemed to be waiting for his answer. 'It was as simple as that. Anyway, I've remembered now that I threw the empty packet away yesterday.' The colour in her cheeks seemed to be a permanent fixture, heightening Joshua's curiosity, she felt sure.

Heavens, it was months since they had talked as much as this—and she wished they weren't talking now!

'What was it?' he asked softly. 'Perhaps I have some I can let you have.'

She shook her head. 'I don't think so.'

'Tell me and maybe——'

'No!'

His eyes narrowed at her uncontrollable outburst. 'What was it, Joanna?' His tone was inflexible, demanding an answer this time.

Her head went back in anger, her expression resentful. 'What do you think it was?'

'I have no idea.' He spoke deceptively low, the hard determination of his jaw belying that tone. 'Tell me.'

It was a command, not a request, and Joanna knew it. If only she hadn't upset that medicine bottle!

'It wasn't drugs, was it, Joanna?' he rasped at her continued silence.

'Drugs?' she repeated astoundedly, her eyes wide with indignation at the suggestion.

'You've been very withdrawn lately——'

'Not because I'm some sort of pill-popper!' She was outraged even at the thought of it.

Joshua sighed. 'I didn't mean those sort of drugs. I know you weren't sleeping well several months ago, I wondered if you were still taking something to help you sleep.'

'And then something to help me wake up again, and something else to give me a little energy, and then——'

'That will do, Joanna!' he told her coldly, only the erratic pulse in his jaw telling of his own rising anger. 'I wasn't implying that at all. I simply wondered if you were taking the sleeping tablets the doctor gave you.'

'No, I'm not. But I was looking for some pills,' she met his gaze with defiant challenge. 'My birth-control pills!'

For a moment he looked stunned, then his expression became as deadpan as usual. 'You're still taking those?' he bit out.

'Yes.'

'Why?'

She gasped. 'Because—Well, because we're married. And——'

'And we haven't slept together in months,' he derided with bitterness, walking to the bedroom door in long strides. 'Or is it years?' he muttered as he left the room.

Joanna fell back against the pillows with an anguished groan, relieved that Joshua hadn't pursued the subject any further.

It wasn't *years* since they had made love, but it was almost a year since Joshua had even wanted to try to make love to her!

CHAPTER TWO

Poor Joshua, he should never have had a wife like her; he would probably never have even considered it if she hadn't pursued him so relentlessly, would probably never even have noticed her if she hadn't made sure he had.

The holiday in Canada with her parents had been part of a few months' holiday together before she went to finishing school in Switzerland during the summer, her mother insisting that she had to learn to ski before she went there, sure that all the other girls would be able to do so and Joanna would feel the odd one out.

So while her mother and father spent the days with another couple they had befriended at the ski complex in Banff, Joanna spent her days travelling up to the nearby Mount Norquay learning to ski on the nursery slopes.

The first few days were great fun, spent with a family of five, two teenage girls, a boy, and their parents as they too attempted to find their feet in the skis that seemed to have a life of their own. They all had a hilarious time, and it wasn't until her parents asked how she was getting on that Joanna realised she should get down to some serious lessons.

After that her progression was very rapid, and after the first week she was more than ready to progress from the real beginners' slopes to the longer more interesting runs.

Her speedy grasp of the sport might have had something to do with the rather handsome instructor she had, the two of them often meeting in the cafeteria for lunch even after she didn't need his teaching any more.

And then she had seen Joshua, had watched in admiration as the figure in the dark blue ski-suit manoeuvred the most difficult run of all with an ease that still made her look very much the amateur. When the skier had reached the bottom of the run he slowed to a halt inches in front of a laughing redhead, his own austere features breaking into a smile as his arm went casually about the woman's shoulders with a familiarity that spoke of several days' acquaintance at least.

Joanna's attention left the smiling woman to return to that handsome face, taking in everything about the man as he removed the woollen hat that had been keeping him warm, his hair long and dark, his eyes so light a grey they looked almost silver. He moved on his skis as if he had been born on them, kissing the redhead lightly on the mouth before taking the chair-lift back up to the top once again. The woman moved to sit on one of the bench seats outside the cafeteria, her bright red ski-suit obviously just for show as she preferred to spend hours just watching the tall dark man.

And he was worth watching; he became almost an obsession for Joanna. To her amazement, and pleasure, he turned out to have a cabin in the same complex as her parents', and so she saw him often. Not that he noticed her. When he wasn't skiing he was wrapped in the arms of the redhead, and Joanna felt her chagrin grow as a second week passed and all she could do was gaze at him from afar.

Then one day the redhead wasn't waiting at the bottom of the run for him! The first day Joanna saw him at the ski-run on his own she thought perhaps the redhead had decided to spend the day in Banff for a change, but when she didn't put in an appearance for three days in a row Joanna knew the other woman had left, that it had only been a holiday romance after all and not a cosy getaway for two in Canada.

As far as she was concerned it was the ideal opportunity for her to make him aware of her, something she hadn't so far achieved, for all that she had tried to.

And it wasn't so easy now either. He spent all of his days on the most experienced ski-slopes, the ones that she hadn't progressed to yet, disappearing completely in the evenings, making Joanna wonder if he had found yet another lady to share his nights. Unless, like her, he was so exhausted by the physical exertion of a day's skiing that he preferred to go to bed early, alone. She had got over her first initial aching body but still found the pure mountain air made her sleepy in the evenings.

Her parents felt no such inhibitions, spending most of their evenings out at dinner in one of the local restaurants with the other couple, and Joanna's interest quickened one morning as they all lingered over breakfast, listening intently as her mother mentioned the man she herself had become so interested in. It had to be him, she hadn't seen another man here who fitted that description!

'Who *is* that fascinating man I occasionally catch a glimpse of in Banff?' her mother asked her father. 'The tall handsome man sitting alone in the restaurant last night.'

'In the restaurant?' Joanna echoed sharply, her disappointment acute that she had once again chosen to spend the evening alone in the luxury two-bedroomed cabin her parents were renting for their stay here. 'Was he?'

Her mother, looking very attractive in a light blue

cashmere jumper and perfectly matched in colour trousers, gave her a sharp look. 'What do you know about him, darling?'

'Nothing.' She flushed, looking very young with her hair secured at her nape, her face completely bare of make-up, already dressed for another day's skiing. 'I've just seen him about the town too.'

Her father shrugged, a man several years older than than her mother, often giving the appearance of being slightly bemused by his beautiful wife at times. He had prematurely grey hair, was of medium height, retaining the lean masculinity of his youth. 'I have no idea who he is. Does it really matter, Cora?'

She looked irritated by his lack of curiosity. 'I suppose not,' she stood up. 'Although I do think you could show some interest.' She lit a cigarette. 'He's English, you know.'

'So are several other people here,' he shrugged.

'But he's staying right here at the complex,' his wife snapped.

'Then ask the manager who he is,' Joanna's father dismissed.

'I will not!' her mother said indignantly.

Joanna left before she could hear her mother's outraged reply, knowing she wouldn't stand for her husband's uninterested attitude towards the stranger any longer. Well, Joanna had decided that today he was going to stop being a stranger to her!

She took her skis and boots up to Mount Norquay as usual, her mother insisting that she couldn't possibly use the rental gear available, that she must have all her own equipment, even though the whole thing had cost a complete fortune. But money had never bothered her parents, and Joanna had grown up knowing she could have anything she wanted. And now she wanted a tall dark stranger with enigmatic grey eyes that could be silver with amusement and like a storm-tossed sea in anger. She had seen the latter once when one of the young skiers came hurtling down the slope so fast he had lost control and almost ploughed down a young child in his way, only just managing to avoid her at the last moment by falling down. The man with the storm-tossed eyes had verbally ripped into the teenager, the young boy's ears burning red at the justification of the reprimand.

But today Joanna was determined the eyes should be silver, with laughter, for her. She had never been denied anything before, and she had never waited so long for anything before either.

She could hardly believe her luck when she reached the ski area and saw the man was also in the locker-room putting on his boots. And they were completely alone. It was all turning out so beautifully!

She saw him glance over at her, but his interest wasn't held in any way as he once again concentrated on his task. She would make him notice her! And luckily she had just the way.

'Oh damn,' she muttered loudly as she put on her own boots. 'Now what am I going to do?' She spoke as if to herself, but made sure she was loud enough to be heard by the man. She could see him moving towards her out of the corner of her eye, and was amazed at how easily he could move in the restrictive boots, always feeling ungainly in them herself until she had her skis on. But he suffered no such inhibitions, he moved easily and smoothly. Joanna looked up as if surprised to see him there. 'Oh, hello, I thought I was alone,' she smiled at him warmly.

He didn't smile back. 'Anything I can do to help?' His voice was deep and husky, and as her mother had said, he was English.

She straightened, overwhelmed by the sexual magnetism of him now that she was this close to him, realising that he was older than she had thought, must be in his early thirties at least, that he smelt of tangy cologne and sandalwood soap. 'I——' she wet her lips nervously. 'One of the straps on my boot has broken. Do you happen to have a spare?' She ignored the spare straps that were burning a hole in the side of her carryall.

'I think so, yes,' he nodded, going back to his own bag and coming back with a blue strap. 'Will this do?' He held it out to her.

'I'm sure it will,' she confirmed huskily. 'Would you mind putting it on for me?'

Dark brows rose beneath the blue woollen hat, but he made no demur, bending down to fit the strap easily, clipping the clasp into place. 'All right?'

'Er—Could you tighten it a little for me?' As he bent forward so did she, her long blonde hair softly brushing the hardness of his cheek.

He glanced up at her, his eyes silvery grey. 'Would you mind . . .?' He brushed her hair away.

Joanna sat back, sighing her chagrin, trying another approach. 'I've watched you ski,' she told him with breathless admiration. 'You're very good.'

'Thank you. Better?' He sat back on his heels, the blue insolated suit fitting tautly to his muscular body.

She blinked. 'Better . . .? Oh—oh yes,' she blushed, making a show of testing the comfort of the boot. 'Thank you.'

He nodded and stood up. 'Then if you'll excuse me . . .'

'Of course.' Once again she smiled, her eyes almost the colour of violets. 'And thank you once again, Mr——?'

'Radcliffe,' he drawled. 'Joshua Radcliffe.'

'Joanna Proctor,' she returned invitingly, looking at him beneath lowered lashes.

'Miss Proctor,' he acknowledged curtly, and instantly left the locker-room.

So much for getting him to notice her! Oh, he had noticed her, all right, and just as soon dismissed her, she thought indignantly. Well, Joshua Radcliffe was about to find out that she only became all the more determined when something was constantly denied her.

But he seemed equally determined to ignore her, barely acknowledging her cheery greeting and hand-waves if they should 'happen' to meet. The day she stopped him to return the strap was the day he couldn't just walk away from her.

It was lunchtime, and the cafeteria was crowded as Joanna pushed her way through to the vacant seat next to Joshua, hardly able to believe her luck as she glanced round the room. He had almost finished his coffee and sandwich, but she hurried to the seat before he could leave.

'May I?' She looked down at him expectantly, knowing the light blue ski suit she wore showed off the slenderness of her figure and deepened the colour of her eyes.

His shrug wasn't encouraging. 'I think it's a question of sit where you can today.'

Not very encouraging at all. And she was very conscious of the other couple sitting at the table as she put her fruit yoghurt and coffee on the table before disposing of the tray, smiling as she sat down next to Joshua Racliffe. 'I'm glad I ran into you today,' she told him breathlessly.

Puzzlement flickered briefly in the dark grey eyes, one brow raised in query. 'You are?'

Her confidence wavered for a moment, although she quickly recovered. 'Yes. I have a new strap for you.' She had been walking about with the strap zipped in her pocket for days in the hope that she would be able to use just such an occasion to sit and talk to him.

'New strap?' he frowned.

'Yes, I——' The man didn't even remember her, there was not a flicker of recognition in the stormy depths of his eyes! She reached up a hand to release her hair from the restrictive hat, its honey blondeness cascading down her back. 'I'm Joanna Proctor, we met in the locker-room the other day,' she prompted as he still looked puzzled. Well, no one had ever accused her of being defeatist!

'Ah yes, Miss Proctor.' His words were obviously spoken out of politeness, still no recognition in his expression.

She didn't know what to say now, and was glad of the diversion of the other couple leaving to shield her dented ego. Luckily the lunchtime rush was over now, so she had Joshua to herself. But he appeared to be getting ready to leave too, picking up his gloves and ski-goggles.

'I have a new strap for you here.' She unzipped her pocket and handed it to him. 'I bought it in town.'

He made no effort to take it. 'There was really no need——'

'Of course there was,' she insisted softly. 'You were kind enough to lend me one of yours, the least I can do is replace it with a new one.'

He shrugged. 'If you insist.' He took the strap and pushed it carelessly into his pocket.

'Oh, I do,' she nodded eagerly. 'Er—could I buy you another cup of coffee?' she asked desperately as he seemed about to get up and leave.

He froze in the action of standing, looking down at her slowly. 'Are you in the habit of buying strange men coffee?' His voice was icy.

She laughed nervously, 'No, I'm not in the habit of doing it,' and here was a man who obviously didn't appreciate the feminine prerogative of making the first move. Or did she mean *moves*—so far she seemed to have done all the chasing. And the man was making it very difficult for her to catch him. 'And I wouldn't call you strange,' she added mischievously.

The eyes flickered silver, although his expression remained stern. 'How old are you?' he rasped.

'How old——?' She was taken aback by the question.

'Yes,' he bit out grimly. 'How old?'

Joanna tentatively touched the tip of her tongue to her lips. 'Er—twenty,' she lied, meeting his gaze unflinchingly.

For a moment he said nothing, then his mouth twisted into a mocking smile. 'And I suppose you've been tempting men since you were in your cradle?' he mused.

He was actually flirting with her! 'Not exactly,' she grinned.

All humour left him, leaving his face more austere than usual. 'That's probably because you haven't left it yet!' And with this abrupt comment he left her.

How could he do that to her, how could he flirt with her one second and treat her like a child the next! Well, it wasn't fair, and she was far from beaten yet.

He didn't put in an appearance for the next three days. The first day she didn't worry too much—after all, he didn't have to spend all his time skiing. But by the third day she began to suspect that he had left Banff, and Canada, to go back to wherever he came from. She cursed herself for not taking better advantage of her chances, knowing she would never again meet a man as fascinating as Joshua Radcliffe.

She moped about the cabin for the next two days, losing interest in the holiday that to many would be the highlight of a lifetime, no longer wishing to ski now that the possibility of seeing Joshua was gone. But finally it was her parents' promptings that persuaded her to go back to Mount Norquay, utterly bored by Greg's attempts to flirt with her, no longer interested in the ski-instructor when she had known the effect of a real man.

And then she saw a familiar navy-blue-clad figure skiing easily down from the top of the mountain—she would recognise that lithe figure anywhere. Joshua hadn't left after all! Suddenly the day took on a new glow, even Greg's conversation seeming interesting, although she was relieved when he excused himself to take his next class. Joshua was still here, and this time she didn't intend to let him disappear, possibly for good, without making some sort of impression on him.

The tangled mess of arms, poles, legs, and skis wasn't quite what she had in mind, but it achieved its objective!

She had watched Joshua go up in the chair-lift once again and had tried to time her descent from one of the small slopes to coincide with the time he too reached the bottom. Unfortunately she spent so much time watching how well he skied that she forgot her own control, suddenly realising she was heading straight for him. It was too late to do more than close her eyes and hope there would be no broken bones.

They met with a crunch of bodies, the force of it knocking all the breath from Joanna's body, leaving her lying on the ground gasping, her legs and skis completely entangled with Joshua's as he lay panting beside her.

He struggled to sit up, brushing the powdered snow from his goggles, finally removing them altogether to look down at her. 'Joanna!' he bit out gruffly. 'Are you all right?' His eyes narrowed as she didn't move.

Her eyes flickered open and she felt slightly dazed, although the fact that he had remembered her name did a lot to help her feel better. 'I——' She seemed to be having trouble talking, completely winded by the fall.

He bent over her now, concern etched into his pale face. 'Are you hurt?' he repeated in a rasping voice.

Was she hurt? She tentatively moved all her limbs, feeling not the slightest twinge, although she knew from experience that she would probably be bruised and aching tomorrow. But if she told Joshua she was all right now would he just get up and leave? She daren't risk it.

She grimaced. 'My wrist hurts.'

His gaze instantly moved down her body. 'Which one?'

Joanna held up her right arm. 'This one.'

'Hm,' his mouth was tight. 'Well, you haven't broken it, or you wouldn't be able to move it that freely.'

Mistake number one! She adopted what she hoped was a pained expression. 'It does hurt quite a lot, though, Joshua.' She saw his face darken at her casual use of his name. Well, she was damned if she would call him Mr Radcliffe!

'Probably just a sprain,' he mumbled, bending down to free himself from his ski, the other one having come loose as he fell and was lying several feet away.

'*Just* a sprain?' she repeated indignantly.

The corners of his mouth quirked into a smile. 'I'm sure it doesn't feel trivial to you, but when I had visions of a broken leg at least, a sprained wrist seems quite mild by comparison.'

'Well, I'm glad about that!' She struggled to sit up without the use of her right hand, determined to carry out the pretence now that she had started it.

'No, you aren't,' he smiled. 'But I hope you'll forgive me for what must seem like callousness. I just didn't intend going home from here leaving a string of broken bodies behind me.'

Only broken hearts, she thought dreamily. She had fallen under his spell once again as he smiled at her, wouldn't have cared if she had broken her leg, not if he came to the hospital to visit her. But she hadn't broken anything, she knew that, even the hurt wrist was just an excuse to stop him getting up and walking away from her.

'Here, let me.' He moved to her aid as she struggled to unclasp her skis, the lock proving too stiff for her, his hand lightly brushing hers as he took over the task, although he seemed unaware of the almost electric shock that surged through her. 'There,' he straightened. 'Now let's see if you can stand up. Then I think we'd better move from here, we seem to be in the way,' he said dryly as yet another skier manoeuvred past them.

With the aid of his arm about her waist Joanna was able to get unsteadily to her feel, more sure than ever that she was going to feel the bruising tomorrow. And the hardness of Joshua's body as he pressed her to his side didn't help the shaking of her legs or the racing of her pulse-rate.

'I'll drive you back to the cabins,' he told her when they had reached the car park, Joshua somehow managing to keep an arm about her waist and carry their skis and poles in the other—and doing it with ease too! 'I have a rental car,' he explained as he leant the poles and skis against the side of the TransAm while he unlocked the passenger door for her, seeing her seated before attaching the skis to the roof-rack, putting their boots and poles in the boot.

She had seen the gold-coloured car with the brown eagle transfer across its bonnet about the complex, but she hadn't realised it was being driven by this man. 'My mother and father are renting a station wagon,' she told him as he got in beside her.

'So you're here with your parents,' he murmured. 'I wondered.'

'You did?' she gasped.

He nodded. 'They don't ski?'

'Oh yes, they do. But not very often,' she confirmed his next unasked question. 'I didn't see you about at the beginning of the week.' She made the statement into a question.

'That's because I wasn't,' he drawled.

'Oh?' she persisted, wondering if he had spent the time with a woman.

He sighed. 'I went up to Sunshine for a few days,' he named the other ski area at Banff.

Relief flooded through her. 'Any good?'

'Very. But a little more crowded than Norquay.'

He helped her out of the car once they reached the cabins, and Joanna didn't feel it necessary to tell him it was her wrist that was injured, not her leg. She enjoyed having him touch her too much!

But when he took her to his own cabin she felt some of her brash self-confidence leave her. She dated a lot when she was at home, but they were usually boys, friends of the family; she had certainly never gone home alone with any of them!

The cabin had the same luxurious layout as the one she was sharing with her parents, the large open-plan lounge and kitchen area, the beautiful stone fireplace in the lounge showing evidence of its recent use, although both the kitchen and lounge were very tidy. She knew there was a bathroom and two bedrooms leading off this, although Joshua took her straight into the lounge, inviting her to sit down on the sofa while he looked at her wrist.

Long sensitive fingers probed her loosely held wrist. 'There's no swelling,' he seemed to speak almost to himself. 'And I can't feel any damage. But I'll bandage it up anyway,' he offered as he saw her mutinous expression. 'It can't do any harm.' He straightened. 'And it may do some good. I won't be a minute.'

Joanna took advantage of his absence to slip out of her ski-suit, her soft wool jumper in the same blue as her eyes and the close-fitting denims she wore beneath the suit warm enough in the centrally heated cabin.

Joshua had removed his own ski-suit when he joined her a few minutes later, the black cords and thick black sweater giving him a satanic look, his warm virility tangible in the confines of the room Joanna's pulse fluttered nervously.

He bandaged her wrist with quick decisive movements, his head bent as he concentrated on the task.

Joanna watched him without interruption, feeling the excitement surge through her. As if her pulse had leapt beneath his fingertips he looked up at her, his eyes narrowing as she blushed, her hair once again released to cascade down her back. 'Er—very professional,' she felt compelled to say something, looking down at the perfectly bandaged wrist to hide the flare of desire she felt sure must be in her eyes.

'It should be,' he drawled. 'I'm a doctor.'

'Oh,' trust her! 'Where in England do you practise?' she asked interestedly.

He looked up at her unblinkingly. 'Why do you want to know?'

She swallowed hard, knowing by the hardness in his eyes that she was being too obvious again. 'I just— wondered,' she said lamely. 'It must be an interesting profession.'

'It is,' he nodded abruptly, securing the bandage. 'And I have a practice in London.'

London. Well, at least they lived in the same city! Although she would be leaving for Switzerland at the end of the summer. Still, that was months away. She had his name and the fact that he worked in London. There couldn't be that many Dr Joshua Radcliffes in town.

He looked up at her once again. 'How does it feel?'

'It——? Oh—fine.' She blushed as she realised he was talking about the bandage. 'Your patients must feel very safe with you,' she added softly, meeting his gaze in challenge.

He was still down on his haunches in front of her. 'And you?' he prompted huskily. 'Do you feel—safe with me?'

Her breath caught in her throat at the sudden warmth in his eyes. 'No.'

'No?' He quirked dark brows mockingly.

Delicate colour warmed her cheeks at the way he was deliberately tormenting her, her mouth tightening defiantly. He wouldn't be amused by her, he wouldn't! 'No,' she said determinedly, bending her head to put her mouth against his.

Because of the precariousness of his position the assault knocked him off balance, his hands coming out to grasp her arms, both of them tumbling to the floor, the deep-pile carpet and thick rug in front of the fireplace cushioning their fall.

Joshua raised his head, his eyes glittering like a storm-tossed sea as he glared down at her. 'Why, you little——!' His mouth ground down on hers in anger, determined to hurt her.

She had never been kissed with such intimacy before, her mouth parting beneath Joshua's as he probed her lips, ravaging and raping her mouth as she lay stunned in his arms, her inexperience shocked by his sexual attack on her body, his hands beneath the thickness of her jumper now, laying claim to one taut breast, tantalising the nipple with sure fingertips.

'No!' He finally thrust her away from him, breathing heavily as he stood up, the tautness of his thighs telling of his own arousal. He turned away as he saw her gaze on him, raking a hand through his hair. 'I think you'd better leave.'

'But——'

'Joanna!' he warned icily, his back still towards her as he shudderingly brought his body back under control. 'Just go. Now.'

She scrambled to her feet, collecting up her clothes before going to the door. She gave one last longing look in his direction before quietly leaving.

But she was adult enough to realise that his anger had mainly been directed at himself, for his response to her. Her own body ached from her pleasure in his rough caresses, and she was determined that she would know that desire again.

Joanna's thoughts came agonisingly back to the present as she heard the slamming of the Rolls' door outside, knowing that Joshua was home. The clock at her bedside told her it was almost eleven. Joshua was later than he usually was, her own time since his departure being spent reliving the time they had met and she had fallen in love. Because she had fallen in love, during that first kiss.

She got to her feet now, hobbling into the bathroom

to empty the cold scented water she had forgotten she had run as she became lost in thoughts of the past.

She was in bed reading a magazine when she heard Joshua coming up the stairs, knowing he must have seen the light on in her room, her windows facing the front of the house. Her face was a polite mask as his knock sounded on her bedroom door, and he entered immediately afterwards.

He looked even more tired than he had earlier tonight, sharpening Joanna's suspicion as to the reason for the tiredness, although she didn't ever remember lovemaking tiring him in the past.

He didn't make the curt goodnight at the door as he usually did, and Joanna stiffened as he came in to sit on the side of her bed. 'How is your foot now?' he enquired softly.

She put her magazine down, her hands clasping together to stop their trembling. This situation reminded her too much of the time she had pretended injury to her wrist, swallowing hard as she remembered the way he had kissed her then. 'It's fine,' she dismissed, just wanting him to leave.

'Sure?' he frowned, looking all of his thirty-seven years.

'Yes!' Her tone was sharp with tension.

His eyes took on the look of a storm-tossed sea as he continued to look at her, his breathing suddenly ragged. She had learnt during their married life together that it wasn't only anger that made his eyes go that colour, that physical desire produced the same effect. It was the latter he was feeling now.

He confirmed her suspicions as he groaned low in his throat. 'God, Joanna, I——'

'No!' She recoiled away from him even as his hands tightened on her arms.

'*Yes*, Joanna,' he bit out grimly. 'Tonight it has to be yes!'

His mouth claimed hers, parting her lips as he bent her to his will, kissing her with an intimacy she thought forgotten. His hands moved feveredly over her body from her hip to her breast, lingering over the latter, tracing the outline of the nipple through the silk of her nightgown, pushing the strap of the gown down as his mouth moved to claim her bare breast.

'No!' she looked up at him with wild eyes. 'I don't want to!' She pushed his hands away from her.

Joshua was breathing heavily as he raised his head, refusing to be pushed off as he pinned her down to the bed. 'You never do,' he ground out. 'But *I* do,' he told her fiercely.

Her eyes glittered her rejection of him. 'Then go and see your little receptionist. But don't come to me!'

His eyes narrowed as he slowly moved up and away from her. 'What's that supposed to mean?' he rasped.

Her mouth twisted, she pulled herself up the pillow now that the danger had passed, straightening the bedclothes about her with a calm she was far from feeling. It was a long time since she and Joshua had discussed anything on such a personal level, and she wasn't sure she was ready for it yet.

'Joanna!' he prompted hardly at her silence.

She sighed, her head back defiantly. 'You know *exactly* what I mean, Joshua, so let's not play games. If you choose to have an affair with your receptionist then that's your business, but don't come to me after you've been with her.'

'I've been working——'

'I think the whole of London is aware of the "work" you've been doing in the evenings lately,' she said contemptuously.

He breathed angrily, his mouth tight. 'In other words, your mother has been listening to one of her cronies again,' he derided harshly. 'No wonder she was concerned about you! When will you learn not to listen to gossip, Joanna?'

She flushed at the rebuke. 'This wasn't gossip, and you know it. And my mother actually defended you,' she told him angrily. 'She thinks a man is entitled to "stray", as long as his wife finds out in time and puts a stop to it,' she added disgustedly.

'But you don't want to do that, do you, Joanna?' he taunted hardly. 'Because if you did that you would have to share a bed with me yourself.'

'Does this mean you admit to having an affair with Angela Hailey?'

'I admit nothing—but I'm not denying it either,' he added softly, too softly. 'Does that give you an excuse to keep denying me access to your bed, and your body?'

'I don't need an excuse!' she snapped, two bright spots of colour in her cheeks.

'No,' he agreed heavily, beginning to pace the room. 'I realise that.' He stopped his pacing to glare down at her. 'Just why the hell did you marry me, Joanna?' he asked wearily.

She looked down at her hands. 'You know why,' she mumbled.

'Tell me!' he ordered tightly.

Her head went back at the aggression in his tone, throwing back the bedclothes to stand up, her body tense with anger as she faced him across the room. 'Because I was eighteen, terrified, and carrying *your* child!'

CHAPTER THREE

As she watched him his face became a shuttered mask, all emotion erased, his eyes the only part of him that showed he hadn't turned to stone, fires leaping and dying amidst the stormy sea.

She wanted to take the words back, to say she was sorry—but it wouldn't have been true. They both knew they would never have thought of marriage between them if it weren't for the reasons she had stated. She was just honest enough, after all this time, to admit it.

'So now I know,' he finally murmured flatly.

'Yes,' she sighed. 'Joshua——'

He walked to the door with long strides. 'I'm too tired to discuss this any further tonight,' he rasped.

'But you do realise we have to talk, that we can't go on like this indefinitely?' She refused to let him leave with things as they were, knew that after tonight she just couldn't go on living like this. To live as virtual strangers was one thing, but Joshua had almost forced himself on her tonight. She couldn't bear the thought of that happening again.

'I realise we—have to talk,' he conceded distantly. 'But not now.'

'Of course.' Her mouth twisted. 'You're tired.'

'Yes,' he bit out, 'I am. I'll see you in the morning.'

'When we'll talk?' she persisted.

'When we'll—talk,' he nodded abruptly, quietly leaving the room.

For the first time in a year Joanna allowed the tears

to fall, felt each shuddering sob rip through the slenderness of her body, crumpling down on to the bed.

She cried until she was sure there couldn't be any tears left inside her, until she felt weak and drained, had no strength to withstand the memories that once again flooded her mind, memories of her time together with Joshua five years ago.

Eighteen and pregnant . . . Yes, that had been her.

Her pursuit of Joshua after that day in his cabin had been even more intense than before, although he gave every impression of not noticing she existed, cutting her dead a couple of times when she attempted to talk to him. But she hadn't given up, she was so determined he would notice her— and that he wouldn't dismiss her this time either. And with the end of her holiday nearing she knew she didn't have any time to waste.

Her parents had had no idea of her interest in Joshua Radcliffe, had believed that if she was attracted to anyone it was to the young ski instructor Greg. Joanna didn't disabuse them of that fact, knowing they would never approve of Joshua for her, his maturity and the experience in his face telling their own story.

By the last day of her holiday Joanna was feeling desperate, knowing she had to do something, anything, to get his attention. Finally she used her injured wrist as an excuse once again, her parents being out at a parting dinner with the couple they had become so friendly with during their stay Joanna refused to accompany them, waiting until they were safely on their way before going over to Joshua Radcliffe's cabin.

The lights were on inside, and she hoped that meant he was at home. If he wasn't she would never see him again, knew she couldn't possibly go and see him in London if she parted from him the way she had three days ago. He had told her to go then, and he had meant it.

A knock on the cabin door elicited some movement inside, and she felt her pulse leap at the sight of him as he opened the door. He was dressed for a leisurely evening in front of the fire, his denims old and faded, the black shirt partly unbuttoned down his chest, a fact he seemed aware of as he slowly rebuttoned it under her avid gaze.

His eyes were narrowed as he looked at her. 'Yes?'

'I—er——' She felt tongue-tied now she had actually dared to come here, realising for the first time just how forward that must appear to him. But it hadn't seemed that way to her when she thought of it, and she knew she would have to see it through with the bravado she possessed in abundance. 'My wrist still seems very painful,' she met his gaze unflinchingly as his expression became watchful. 'I wondered if you would take another look as it. As you're a doctor,' she added pointedly.

For a brief moment irritation flared in his eyes, then he nodded, opening the door wider. 'You'd better come in.'

Not exactly the most eager invitation she had ever received, but she accepted anyway, instantly feeling the warmth of the cabin, a gentle snow falling outside, the temperature well below freezing. She gave a pleasurable shiver as the warmth invaded her chilled body.

She bent down to take her boots off, taking care not to use her right hand too much, knowing piercing grey eyes were watching her every move. Almost as if he suspected the whole thing was a ruse!

But of course he couldn't know that. A strained wrist could only really be felt by the injured person, this man couldn't possibly know that the bandage she wore was completely unnecessary.

'Ooh, what a lovely fire!' Her face glowed as she

followed him into the lounge, warming her hands in front of the blazing logs.

His dark brows rose. 'Don't you have one in your own cabin?'

She had said the first thing that came into her head as she entered the room, realising now how stupid it had been. He would only have to look out of the window to see the smoke billowing out of her chimney to know she did indeed have a fire. 'Oh yes,' she nodded. 'But it isn't as nice as this one,' she added lamely.

'Indeed?' He looked sceptical. 'Well, you'd better let me take a look at it.'

She frowned. 'The fire?'

'Your wrist,' he derided.

Hot colour flooded her cheeks. 'Oh yes.' She held it out to him to examine.

Joshua's mouth twisted. 'Perhaps you would like to take your coat off and make yourself comfortable on the sofa. If your wrist still hurts that badly after all this time I'd better take a thorough look at it. Maybe I missed a fracture last time.'

Joanna unzipped her anorak, slipping her arms out of it with his help, pulling off the woollen hat she had pulled down over her ears, knowing the navy blue jumper and matching cords suited her slenderness, the jumper making her hair appear blonder than ever.

This time when he probed her wrist he did so with a concentration that left her gasping.

'That hurts?' He looked up sharply as he heard her indrawn breath.

She swallowed hard. It hadn't hurt at all; his touch on her flesh had fired her senses, and she hadn't been able to hold back her gasp of pleasure. 'Just a little.' She moistened her dry lips, this time unable to meet his gaze.

He placed her hand gently down on her thigh and stood up. 'I'm sure it's just a sprain,' he said tersely. 'It will hurt for a while.'

She nodded, her nose wrinkling enchantingly as she looked up at him. 'I just thought I would make sure. What's that delicious smell?' she asked eagerly, her mouth watering at the lovely aroma wafting over from the kitchen area.

'Spare ribs,' he supplied the answer with a dark frown.

She smiled. 'They smell lovely.'

Joshua seemed to hesitate, a hundred different emotions flickering across his face at the same time, and none of them definitely discernible. 'Would you like to join me for dinner?' he asked abruptly.

'Oh, I couldn't——'

'You could,' he drawled derisively. 'Please. I have more than enough for two.'

Her eyes glowed her pleasure. 'Well, if you're sure . . .'

'I am,' he nodded. 'You can make the salad dressing while I finish cooking the ribs.'

She couldn't have been happier, and if they should happen to touch by accident as they finished preparing the dinner together in the kitchen area then she didn't mind at all. Joshua's expression remained enigmatic, but he didn't seem to mind too much either.

'Will your parents be wondering where you are?' he asked as they served the meal.

She shook her head. 'They're out.'

'I see,' he frowned. 'You seem to have been on your own a lot the last few weeks.'

She shrugged, carrying the plates over to the breakfast-bar. 'I'm hardly a child that they feel they have to entertain me.'

'No,' he sat down next to her, his thigh briefly touching hers before he moved slightly away. 'How old did you say you were?' he quirked dark brows.

'Er—twenty,' she suddenly remembered. God, she was hopeless at lying—she could never remember what she had said! And she had a feeling this man knew that. His next words confirmed it.

'What does that mean?' he derided. 'That you're one month over nineteen?'

At least he hadn't guessed the real truth! 'Something like that,' she smiled her relief. 'You're a good cook, Joshua,' she changed the subject.

'And you make a good salad dressing,' he said lightly. 'I'm roasting marshmallows for dessert,' he grinned, instantly looking younger.

It sounded revolting, but Joanna found it delicious when she tried it later, the inside of the marshmallow all soft, the outside crisper, with a slightly burnt taste. 'Mm, they're lovely.' She ate another one off the end of her fork, about her fifth, she thought.

Joshua sat at her side in front of the fire, both their faces glowing from sitting so close to the flames, Joshua sitting cross-legged on the floor, his bare feet under his legs. 'Here, have this one,' he held out his fork to her. 'I've had enough.'

There was something very intimate about him feeding her, and as she bent forward to take the marshmallow her gaze locked and held with his, the pulse beating erratically in his cheek telling her that he too was affected by the provocation of the moment.

'Joshua——'

'Let's go and load the dishwasher,' he stood up, pulling her to her feet, 'and then I think you'd better go back to your own cabin.'

She didn't want to leave yet, had no intention of

going yet, not until she had known the fulfilment of that promise in his eyes during that unguarded look. He couldn't look at her like that, with naked desire one minute, and then treat her like a child the next.

'Could I have a coffee first?' she asked huskily once they had loaded the dishwasher in silence. 'My parents won't be back yet and——'

'All right, a coffee,' he agreed abruptly. 'Go and sit down and I'll make us some.'

'No, let me——' She broke off as her body collided with his, the tension between them a tangible force now, Joshua's hands rough on her arms as he steadied her.

He looked down at her in silence for several long minutes, his breathing deep and ragged, his gaze locked on the parted pinkness of her mouth. Finally he thrust her away from him. 'All right,' he bit out, 'you make it. I like mine strong,' he added abruptly.

'So do I.' She sounded almost timid, aware that this had stopped being a challenge, that Joshua was now as deeply aware of her as she was of him, and that he knew much more about appeasing that sudden flare of desire than she did. Suddenly this was no longer a game.

It was relatively easy for her to find the makings for coffee, and apprehensive glances at Joshua as he sat in the lounge revealed a stony expression. His face remained grim as she carried in the tray of coffee, although he sat forward on the sofa to make room for the tray on the table as she came through with it.

'Black and sweet,' he responded tersely to her query. 'It's as good as a cold shower,' he added derisively.

Joanna sat down beside him, her eyes downcast as she poured his coffee, adding a liberal amount of sugar before pouring her own unsweetened brew.

'Why me, Joanna?' he asked suddenly.

Her lids flew open in surprise, then she quickly lowered them again as she saw the mockery in his gaze.

'Why not the young ski-instructor who can't take his eyes off you?' he continued softly. 'Or one of the other young men here who only needed a word or look of encouragement for you?'

She tentatively moistened her lips, her lashes fanning her cheeks. 'I don't know what you mean——'

'Oh yes, you do,' he taunted huskily. 'Ever since that first day you saw me with Mari you've——'

'Mari?' she echoed in a puzzled voice.

'My young American friend with the red hair,' he drawled derisively. 'Every since that first day I've been aware of you watching me, of always being where I am.'

She was stricken that he had noticed so much. 'And laughing at me, I suppose,' she choked. 'With her!'

His face darkened, his mouth tautening to a thin line. 'Neither of us laughed at you, Joanna. I doubt Mari was even aware of your interest.'

Tears glistened in her eyes as she realised what a fool she had made of herself in his eyes. He probably even knew there had never been any injury to her wrist. God, she wanted to die!

'Joanna——'

She sprang to her feet, so embarrassed she wanted to just go away and hide—at the very least to be alone to lick her wounds of humiliation!

'Joanna!' Joshua stood up too, grasping her shoulders. 'I'm not trying to hurt you——'

'Aren't you?' she choked. 'It seems that way to me!'

'And how does this seem?' he enquired gently, bending his head enough to softly claim her lips with his own. His breathing was very ragged when he finally lifted his head. 'I'm trying very hard to resist you, Joanna, but you aren't making it easy for me.'

Her mouth tingled from the pressure of his, her misery forgotten as her whole body came alive beneath his touch. 'Did you resist Mari?' she asked.

He frowned. 'What does——'

'Did you?' she persisted softly.

'No,' he admitted ruefully. 'But we were both willing for a holiday—romance.'

'Affair,' Joanna amended scornfully.

'Affair, then,' he gave a dismissive shrug. 'Although it wasn't even that. We'll probably never meet again, in fact, I'm sure we won't.'

'Neither will we after tomorrow.'

'Tomorrow?' he echoed sharply, suddenly tense. 'Are you leaving tomorrow?'

'Yes,' she sighed. 'Does that make a difference to how you feel about me now?'

'It shouldn't,' he said grimly. 'But somehow it does. I'm going to miss your little heart-shaped face peeping at me from beneath a bright woolly hat. Maybe if we'd had more time together, could have become friends . . .'

'Maybe what?' Joanna's tone showed her exasperation with such an enigmatic statement.

Joshua shrugged his broad shoulders, moving to thrust his hands in his trouser pockets. 'Just maybe.'

For a few brief moments, she had felt as if she were on the brink of some momentous discovery, had felt Joshua being pulled to her in spite of himself. And now he was more or less asking her to leave again.

'Joshua, no one can live on maybes,' there was pleading in her voice. 'It's my last evening here, and——'

'And you want something to remember the holiday by!' he ground out viciously. 'A night in a man's bed— any man, that you can look back on in connection with this holiday?'

She shook her head in bewilderment. 'No. I——'

'Because if that's all you want, Joanna, you can have it!' He pulled her fiercely against him, his mouth a brutal assault on her unprepared lips. 'You've been asking for this for three weeks now!' He pushed her down on to the rug in front of the fire, swiftly covering her body with his. 'Well, now you can damn well have it!' His hand reached out to switch off the main light, leaving the room bathed in a red glow. 'By firelight, no less!' he taunted hardly, throwing off his shirt to reveal his deeply bronzed chest. 'I hope this proves to be as memorable as you thought it would, Joanna,' he muttered before his mouth claimed hers again.

By his tone and manner she had been expecting more aggression; instead she got such tenderness that her very bones seemed to melt. With a confidence she couldn't deny Joshua touched all the unguarded places no other man had probed, and it wasn't long before she was naked beneath him, eagerly urging the joining of his body with hers.

'A night to remember, Joanna,' he slowed down the pace with languorous kisses, 'for both of us.'

His lips began to know all of her body now, first one breast, then the other, sliding down to kiss her inner thigh, and Joanna's gasp of surprise quickly turned to one of pleasure as Joshua's mouth ignited a flame of passion so overwhelming her body began to shudder as little time-bombs went off inside her. Joshua was not satisfied until she was sated.

'Now me.' His kissed her on the lips before lying down beside her, an expectant look on his aroused passion-filled face.

She still felt dizzy from the pleasure that had racked her body, knowing only that he wanted her to make love to him in the same way he had just done to her.

With the knowledge of Eve she soon had him gasping his own pleasure, knowing a sense of elation that she could arouse and fulfil him in return, murmuring a protest as he refused to let her take him over the edge.

But their lovemaking was far from over. Joshua aroused her even more quickly the second time, her body eager for his as he lay between her parted thighs, the probe of his manhood meeting only a little resistance, although it was enough to cause his eyes to widen in surprise.

Joanna allowed him no time for questions, moving against him in a rhythm that he soon had to follow, the explosion of their bodies as they reached a simultaneous climax making Joanna wonder if they had both died and gone to heaven.

Joshua was heavy above her, although his caresses soothed the sporadic trembling of her body, the pleasure having been almost too much to bear, her whole body bathed in a flow of ecstasy still.

Finally he raised his head to look down at her, a question in the icy grey depths of his eyes as his body left her, leaning on his elbow to gaze down at her flushed face.

'It was mine to give,' she told him heatedly before he could say anything.

He sighed, swallowing convulsively. 'That's true. But——'

'And I gave it to the man I wanted to!'

'Joanna——'

She pushed away from him, standing up, like a young goddess as she stood naked in front of him, her body having all the allure of the woman she had just become, the firelight picking out every contour and curve. 'I don't regret what just happened,' her voice shook with emotion. 'Not for an instant!'

Joshua closed his eyes for a moment, a fire burning in their depths as he opened them again. 'Neither do I.' He slowly stood up, his body tanned and glistening with sweat from their lovemaking in front of the fire. He gave a slow smile. 'Let's go and take a bath together in the king-size tub.' His arm came about her waist.

Joanna moistened her lips nervously. 'And afterwards?'

He laughed softly. 'Afterwards—or during—we can make love again.'

They did manage to wait until they reached the bedroom, although not until they had dried themselves, their wet gleaming bodies soon drying under the heat of their passion.

Joanna had never felt so happy in her entire life, and she fell asleep in Joshua's arms, her head resting on his shoulder, more sure than ever that she loved this man.

She woke with a start, unsure of her surroundings for a moment, or the solid wall of chest beneath her cheek. Joshua murmured in his sleep, pulling her closer to the hard arousal of his body.

'Want you,' he murmured drowsily, his eyes opening wide as he too came fully awake. 'God, Joanna, I want you again,' he groaned.

'I have to leave,' she told him softly. 'It's after eleven, my parents are expecting me to be at home when they get back.'

'Not yet.' The storm-tossed eyes pleaded with her. 'Just a little while longer, Joanna. Please!'

His hands were already caressing her body with an intimacy that she didn't have the willpower to resist, and she was weak to the pleading in his voice, groaning her capitulation.

It was over an hour later before she left him, hurrying back to her parents' cabin, carrying the warm glow of Joshua's lovemaking with her.

That wasn't all she had carried with her from that night! Just six weeks later, on their return from their stay in Florida, Joanna knew she carried his child too.

She had woken the morning after their lovemaking with the knowledge that she was leaving Canada today, as her parents were longing for the sunshine of a Florida holiday after all this snow.

They were due to leave for the airport at ten o'clock, and Joanna waited anxiously for Joshua to come and say goodbye to her. He hadn't said he would, but she felt sure he would do so.

By ten she knew he wasn't coming, and burying her pride she ran over to his cabin. Her urgent knock received no reply, and the door was locked when she tried it. Joshua wasn't even here; he had probably just gone skiing as he usually did!

She felt as if the bottom had dropped out of her world. And worst of all, she felt *used*, just another holiday affair to Joshua, like Mari had been. The most humiliating part was knowing that she had been responsible for what happened, that without her determined chasing of him Joshua probably wouldn't have given her a second glance.

The six weeks in Florida had been miserable for her, although her parents had a wonderful time and were unable to understand their daughter's unhappiness. Joanna's heart felt as if a cold weight had settled on it, and she knew that the night that had meant so little to Joshua that he hadn't even taken the trouble to say goodbye to her was the night she had given him her heart.

She completely panicked when she realised she was pregnant, terrified of the reprisals of such a mistake. At first she had tried to deny it to herself, but when she missed yet another period she knew that she was indeed carrying Joshua's child, was just over two months pregnant.

That was it! It *was* his child, not just hers, but his too, and she couldn't go through this alone, didn't want to go through it at all. Joshua was a doctor, he would know what to do for the best.

She had been right about there not being many Joshua Radcliffes in the London telephone book, and only one of them was a doctor—in Harley Street! It had come as a shock to her to realise what an important and distinguished man he was, the lighthearted man enjoying his skiing holiday suddenly turning into an austere Harley Street specialist. Joanna had hesitated about contacting such an important man, but a faint fluttering sensation in her body of the new life forming inside her had her running to the telephone in a panic.

His receptionist proved to be particularly obstructive, the only way Joanna could get to see him being to make an appointment to visit him professionally!

She dressed with care the day she went to his office, finding the waspish receptionist to be Angela Hailey, although she was polite enough as she showed Joanna into the plush waiting-room, with armchairs and furniture more like you would find in a lounge than a doctor's waiting-room.

When twelve o'clock finally came she was shown into the actual surgery, not a second before twelve but not a second after either. Still, the price Joshua's patients were paying for his skills was phenomenal, they should receive this first class treatment.

Joshua was sitting behind an imposing leather-topped desk, a distinctly masculine room, the walls lined with books, the decor brown and cream. His eyes narrowed on her as he invited her to sit down, eyes like a storm-tossed sea in mid-December—and just as cold.

He looked completely alien to the man she had met in Canada, his dark hair cut shorter, revealing several strands of grey among its blackness, the dark grey three-piece suit he wore superbly tailored, as was the white silk shirt beneath, the grey tie looking as if it were made from the same material. He looked exactly what he was, a successful man.

'Joanna,' he greeted her abruptly, his expression cold.

She swallowed hard, beginning to wonder what she was doing here, how this man could possibly help her. She didn't think now that he could. 'Dr Radcl——'

'Mr,' he corrected softly. 'And I seem to remember you called me Joshua the last time we—spoke together,' he drawled.

They had done much more than just talk together, and they both remembered that very well. 'Joshua.' She moistened her lips. 'I—I need your help.'

He seemed to stiffen, although his expression remained bland. 'In what way can I help you?'

How did you tell a man you were expecting his child, and that you were terrified of bringing it into the world? She decided there was no other way but the truth. 'I'm pregnant,' she stated bluntly.

Not even by the blink of an eyelid did he show he was in the least disturbed by what she had just told him. 'Yes?' he finally said distantly, his fingertips beating a soft tattoo on the desktop.

Joanna didn't know what she had expected— outraged denials of the child being his, stunned silence perhaps, but certainly not this coldness and that disturbing tattoo of his fingertips against leather.

'What sort of help do you want from me?' he prompted at her silence.

'I—You're a doctor.'

'Yes?' His voice was even more chilled now.

'Then you must know what to do to—to——'

'Abort it,' he finished coldly. 'Is that why you're here, Joanna? To trade on a night we spent together, demanding I abort your child as payment for that night?'

The words washed over her, and the brutality of what he was saying robbed her of the power of speech. Abortion. He had dared to put into words what she had only dared to think of.

'How did you find me, Joanna?' he rasped suddenly.

'I—It wasn't difficult.'

'And so you thought you would use me to rid yourself of your unwanted child. You're young and healthy, aren't you?'

Her eyes were wide. 'Yes.'

'With no history of illness in your family?'

'None.'

'Then you would expect me to carry out this abortion against all that I believe in?'

She swallowed hard, feeling sicker by the moment. Why was he asking her all these questions—couldn't he see what he was doing to her? 'You're a doctor——'

'I'm more than that, I'm a gynaecologist,' he bit out. 'But I would need more than your aversion to a child to carry out such a task. I take it you *don't* want it?'

'No!' she choked, hating him more and more with each probing question.

He nodded. 'And the father, does he want it?'

She blinked her puzzlement. 'I don't know——'

'Have you tried asking him?' His mouth was twisted contemptuously. 'Or don't you know who he is?' he taunted. 'God, when I made love to you I had no idea you'd turn into a damned wanton! Although your body did promise a sensuality you had only just begun to realise, I remember it haunted me for weeks afterwards,' he murmured, his gaze totally assessing, settling on her already thickening waistline in the loose-fitting yellow sun-dress. 'Have you been to see your own doctor?' he asked slowly, the colour beginning to ebb from his lean cheeks.

Joanna saw the dawning horror in his expression, knew that the truth was beginning to hit him. Until a few minutes ago she hadn't realised he didn't know he was the father. The shock to him seemed to be all the deeper now. 'Yes,' she nodded.

'I—You—How many weeks are you?'

'Eight weeks, one day, and about . . .' she looked at her wrist-watch, her hand shaking, 'about six hours,' she finished jerkily.

Joshua drew in a ragged breath. 'I'm the father.'

'Yes,' she confirmed simply.

He stood up as if in a trance, coming round the desk to pull her strongly to her feet, one of his hands coming to rest on her rounded stomach. Her pregnancy was very obvious against her other slenderness, the only way she had been able to hide her condition from her parents had been to wear loose dresses, although she was aware that already her breasts were getting larger too.

Joshua's hand gently touched her thickening waistline, sensing the new life there. 'You're carrying my child,' he spoke almost in wonder.

Joanna could tell by his reaction to such a thought that 'the father' did indeed want his child!

She pulled away from him at the intimacy of his touch, avoiding his gaze. 'Will you help me now?'

'Yes,' he told her abruptly. 'Although not in the way you want,' he added as his expression brightened. 'You will not harm my child, Joanna. And I mean to make sure you don't.'

'How?' she asked defiantly.

'By marrying you.'

She gasped, her face paling. 'No . . .'

'I know you're very young, that the idea of having a child probably frightens you. But doesn't the idea of an abortion frighten you more?' he rasped.

'Yes!' she choked, the tears starting to fall. 'Yes, of course it does. I want my baby, Joshua, I really want it. But I'm so frightened!'

'You have no need to be now, I shall support you. Have you told your parents?' he queried softly.

'No.' She blew her nose noisily with the snowy white handkerchief he handed her. 'My father would have been around here with a shotgun by now if I had!' she attempted to smile.

Joshua found nothing humorous about the situation, his face was devoid of all expression. 'You're under age?' he asked abruptly.

She moistened her lips, chewing on the bottom one. 'I was eighteen last month,' she revealed, watching the anger flare in his eyes.

'So you were only seventeen in Canada?' He spoke softly, dangerously.

'Yes,' she admitted miserably.

He gave a disbelieving snort. 'You stupid child,' he groaned. 'Stupid, stupid, *stupid*!'

And she had been stupid to marry him. All she had left was a dead child and a dead marriage.

CHAPTER FOUR

DESPITE the bad start to their relationship, marriage to Joshua hadn't been a failure. After all, she was still in love with him, and it soon became obvious once he was her husband that he still desired her.

Her parents had been deeply shocked when Joshua drove her home and told them that the two of them were getting married. Her father had been outraged at the idea, and her mother had told them that Joanna had to go to finishing school first, that if they still wanted to be married then perhaps they might consider giving their permission.

Joshua's answer was to be expected. He was a man in his thirties, a highly qualified specialist, and he wasn't about to be talked down to in that way by anyone. He had told her parents that unless they wanted their grandchild born without a legal father they had better agree now.

Joanna had been glad of his support as the storm broke over her head; she had clutched on to his warm protectiveness as her parents' shocked reactions reverberated around them.

And he had continued to protect her, had arranged the wedding as quickly as possible, making sure that nothing upset her, that her parents understood that two people had created the child she carried, and that any recriminations be directed at him first. One look into his cold grey eyes was enough to silence anyone who dared to be disparaging about Joanna's condition.

Their wedding had taken place within a week of the

decision being made, and even her parents had
attended, their initial objections forgotten as they
recognised a force stronger than themselves. Joanna
and Joshua had spent their honeymoon in Paris, and
despite Joanna's misgivings it had been a honeymoon to
remember. Joshua's lovemaking had given her the glow
of a woman in love, fulfilling her as a woman with
gentleness and passion, never leaving her in any doubt
as to her ability to arouse him in return. But the
honeymoon hadn't lasted for ever, just the two weeks
Joshua could spare at the time, and all too soon they
were back in London, with Joanna the wife of a
brilliant and influential man.

Having been brought up in a house run by servants
she had no trouble in taking control of Joshua's
household, although she knew that at the beginning the
staff resented a child like her becoming mistress of the
house. But Joanna was her mother's daughter, and her
polite but commanding manner soon paid off.

But because of the difference in her age from
Joshua's she became aware of the fact that a lot of
her old friends now seemed childish to her, the fact
that she wasn't just a married lady but pregnant as
well making them more so. Without really being
aware of it she dropped most of her old friends and
adopted Joshua's.

Her marriage to Joshua hadn't been the dismal
failure it could have expected to be, and they were still
sharing a bed and making love the night Lindy was
born. In fact, they often joked afterwards that that had
contributed to her arriving a month earlier than
expected, their passion for each other allowing for no
respite, as fierce as when they were first married.

Joshua had stayed with her during the magic time of
Lindy being born, encouraging, comforting, praising.

And they had both been proud when their new daughter was placed in Joanna's arms.

Those first few weeks after Lindy was born were the happiest Joanna had ever known. The spoilt little girl she had been in Canada was completely gone now, a new maturity in its place. Caring for Lindy filled her with a fierce pride, even the night-time feeds everyone seemed to complain about didn't bother her. In fact, they became more special, because Joshua would share those with her, and would watch with undisguised desire as his child suckled at her breast.

Then came Lindy's six-week-old check-up. Joshua drove them to the clinic for this routine examination. The doctor seemed to spend a long time over it, although he assured Joanna at the time that everything was normal.

A week later he called them and asked them to bring Lindy back in to see him, that he would like to see them all. Joshua seemed terse and preoccupied on the drive there, although it in no way matched the tension Joanna was feeling.

The doctor was a friend of Joshua's, and he explained to them exactly what was wrong with Lindy, but Joanna could only look at her husband, not understanding a word the doctor said to them, only seeing how grey and strained Joshua's face became, his eyes filled with pain.

Her hold on Lindy tightened. 'Could you not—not talk in such technical terms,' she finally choked. 'And tell me what's wrong with my baby!'

'Joanna——'

'Tell me!' She looked frantically from Joshua to the doctor, and then back again. 'You understand what he's saying, so tell me what's wrong with Lindy!'

The doctor touched Joshua's arm in a comforting

gesture. 'I'll leave you two alone to talk. I'm so sorry, if there's anything I can do . . .'

'Thank you,' Joshua accepted gruffly.

Joanna's face was deathly white by this time, knowing there was something terribly wrong with her beautiful Lindy.

'Is she going to die?' she groaned brokenly.

Joshua seemed to pale even more, his breathing ragged. 'I don't know,' he said harshly. 'I just don't know.'

That air of defeat was completely alien to the self-confident man she had married, and she felt her heart plummet. 'What's wrong with her?' Her voice was shrill.

'At the moment just an irregularity in her blood. How serious it is we can't be sure——'

'Then be sure!' she cried. 'Have tests done. Joshua, do something!'

'Patrick is arranging for Lindy to go into hospital for tests right now——'

'No!' She held the baby to her protectively, shaking her head. 'You aren't taking her away from me!'

'Joanna——'

'I said no!' Her eyes were wild.

His hands on her arms calmed her. 'Arrangements are being made for you to stay with Lindy at the hospital,' he told her gently. 'I'm not completely insensitive, Joanna.'

The baby gave a cry of protest at being held so tightly, and Joanna looked down at her daughter with silent tears streaming down her face. Lindy had inherited her father's dark hair, her mother's blue eyes, each tiny feature and limb was perfect. How could there possibly be anything wrong with her!

'She's so small,' Joanna choked. 'So tiny and helpless.'

Joshua's arm came protectively about her shoulders. 'I know, darling. We'll do everything we can, Joanna.'

Everything hadn't been good enough. All the tests, examinations, more tests, more examinations, had proved useless. Their little Lindy was going to die. Maybe not that week, or even that month, it might not even be that year, but she was eventually going to die, and there was nothing they could do to stop it.

Lindy had seemed so normal most of the time, had learnt to crawl at seven months, to walk at eleven months, to get into every conceivable mischief from the time she could pull herself along the floor. On those days, the good days, Joanna couldn't believe there was anything wrong with her daughter.

And then would come the days when Lindy would simply lie on the floor or in a chair, her face pale, her energy all used up, her little body too exhausted to move. Those were the black days for Joanna, the days she knew she was going to lose her daughter.

She did everything for Lindy herself—fed her, clothed her, bathed her, played with her, knowing she was shutting Joshua out of a special and beautiful relationship with his daughter and yet unable to stop herself.

Joshua warned her that such devotion for Lindy twenty-four hours a day would only result in her being ill herself. He was right, and a bout of 'flu put her in bed for a week. Joshua stayed at home during that time to take care of two-year-old Lindy. During that week Joanna had learnt to share her daughter once again, to let Joshua know the fun and love that was Lindy.

Her own relationship with Joshua was still as intimate, his desire for her often taking them into the early hours of the morning. It was after one of these insatiable nights in Joshua's arms that she had sensed something was wrong with Lindy, some sixth sense telling her that all was not well with their daughter.

Joshua had given a protesting groan as she pulled gently out of his arms, padding softly through the darkness to Lindy's room next door to theirs. Lindy didn't seem to be breathing, her face was grey, and Joanna's scream of terror brought Joshua running.

What had followed was still a nightmare in her mind. The ambulance, the bright lights, people running, an emergency-room, a serious-faced doctor gently telling them there had been nothing he could do, no magic spell he could weave to bring Lindy back to them.

It hadn't seemed real to Joanna, that frail little body lying so still and lifeless on the examination couch not looking like her little Lindy at all. Lindy was at home, with her peaches and cream complexion, her mouth curved into that mischievous smile that melted even the hardest heart, her black hair falling in soft curls on to her pillow.

But Lindy hadn't been at home, her small bed was empty, the bedclothes still thrown back, the fluffy white rabbit she loved so much lying on the pillow next to where Lindy's head should have been.

And even then Joanna hadn't cried, had carried on normally throughout the day, seeing her mother's grief as if she were a stranger to her, wondering what on earth she could be crying about so brokenly.

Her illusion of normality hadn't been broken until she lay in bed next to Joshua that night, not seeing the tears on his cheeks, the pain etched into his face, knowing only that their daughter was dead and that he was trying to make love to her!

She had turned on him like a virago, scratching, biting, kicking, and all the time hurling abuse at him, all the pent-up emotion and resentment of the last four years of marriage to him bursting forth in one explosion, only stopping when his palm landed painfully against her cheek.

That had been when pain such as she had never known before had ripped through her heart, Lindy's death becoming a reality in that resounding blow. Then the tears started, hysterical sobbing tears that hadn't stopped until the sleep-giving needle pierced her arm and took her off to oblivion.

Joshua had moved back into his own bedroom during the weeks when Joanna lay grief-stricken in her bed, and when she had slowly begun to face the world again, a slow and painful process, she had cut him out of her life as if they had never been married, their one link in Lindy, the reason they had married at all, now gone for ever.

She got up stiffly from the bed, all the past relived now, only the future stretching out in front of her, and she knew that whatever it held she could no longer remain married to Joshua. Tonight they had overstepped the polite limits they had set for themselves this last year, and there could only be one end to this now.

She was woken the next morning by a tray of tea being placed on her bedside table, and looked up to see, not the maid as she had expected, but Joshua. And he was already dressed and ready for his clinic.

'You overslept,' he told her abruptly. 'It's almost nine o'clock.'

She sat up against the pillows, idly opening the single letter for her that had been placed on the tray. 'I thought we were going to talk today,' she frowned.

He nodded. 'It will have to wait until tonight now. I have my first appointment at nine.'

She chewed on her bottom lip. 'Couldn't it wait? Isn't

what we have to say more important than an appointment?'

Joshua pushed his dark hair from his brow impatiently. 'You know it is.'

'Perhaps it isn't an appointment after all.' Her tone was brittle. 'Can't your mistress do without you for a few hours, Joshua?' she scorned.

Angry colour darkened his lean cheeks. 'Do you think you have any right to behave like a jealous wife?' he rasped.

She drew in an angry breath at the barb. 'Do you think you have the right to flaunt your affair for the whole of London to see?' she hissed.

'The whole of London isn't interested, Joanna,' he derided coldly. 'An affair is too commonplace now-adays. No, I'm sure our sleeping arrangements would be a much more interesting piece of gossip. How many marriages like ours do you think there are, Joanna?' he taunted. 'Not many, I'm sure.'

'You would know more about that than I, Joshua,' she snapped. 'Your patients tell you all these little intimate details of their life.'

He gave her a look that told her of his disgust. 'Not always,' he said tightly. 'And I don't think I've ever come across a woman of twenty-three who doesn't sleep with her husband.'

Joanna plucked nervously at the sheet. 'That's why I would like to talk to you. I——'

'I really don't have the time for this now, Joanna,' he glanced impatiently at his wrist-watch. 'We'll talk tonight.'

'When?' she asked bitterly. 'While Mrs Barnaby serves us dinner, or when you get back from the *clinic* at eleven o'clock at night again?'

His mouth tightened. 'I'm not going back to the

clinic tonight, and we aren't at home to dinner. Have you forgotten we're going to Patrick and Tina's for dinner?'

She had forgotten, she had had too much on her mind to remember that Patrick and Tina Mayor were giving a dinner party tonight. Patrick was the man who had brought Lindy into the world, the man who had had the task of telling her how ill her daughter was. He and his wife Tina had become their very dear friends the last five years, and she and Tina were very close, the two of them being of a similar age; Tina was only twenty-eight.

Nevertheless, she didn't really want to spend a social evening with Joshua tonight; she would rather stay at home and discuss the end of their marriage.

'We have to go.' Joshua seemed to see the refusal in her face. 'I spoke to Patrick only yesterday and told him you were looking forward to seeing Tina again. He said you haven't been over for several weeks,' he frowned.

Joanna shrugged. 'There hasn't been the time.' She moved her letter absently from hand to hand.

'You should always make time for your friends, Joanna.'

She flushed at the rebuke in his tone. 'The way you do?' she snapped.

He gave an impatient sigh. 'I have to go, Joanna. Don't forget to have some breakfast before you go out.'

Her eyes flashed her anger. 'Somewhere during this marriage, Joshua, I grew up,' she bit out. 'I wish you would realise that. Everyone else has!'

His eyes narrowed to grey slits. 'What's that supposed to mean?'

She was breathing deeply in her agitation. 'It means I'm a grown woman now, not a little girl out to impress.'

'And who was easily impressed!'

Her mouth twisted. 'You underestimate yourself, Joshua. Even my mother was attracted to your good looks when we were in Banff.'

'That soon changed,' he derided.

'I think a son-in-law was the last thing she had in mind for you,' Joanna mused, her tension easing a little.

'I don't think she's too thrilled at the thought of you being an author either,' he drawled.

'One book doesn't an author make,' she quipped.

'Your mother told me you'd been asked to write a series of them,' he frowned.

She shook her head. 'I'm not sure I can do that.'

'Why not? You always seemed to have hundreds of "Biwwy stories" to tell Lindy——' he broke off as he saw how pale she had gone at his imitation of the way their daughter had always asked for tales about the mischievous dog. 'I'm sorry,' he said abruptly, turning away. 'I thought after all this time I could talk about— Never mind,' he dismissed. 'I'll be home around seven as usual.'

Joanna wanted to call him back, wanted to tell him that to talk about Lindy was all right, that not to talk or think about her was what hurt the most. But he had already gone, only the masculine smell of his cologne remaining.

It was the first Joshua had spoken about Lindy for a very long time, in fact, it was only the last two days they had done more than exchange pleasantries since the night Lindy died.

The talk about their marriage might have been postponed until after the dinner party tonight, but she wouldn't delay any longer than that; she couldn't live like this any longer. The first 'Billy Boxer' book might only be a beginning, but it was her first step away from dependence on Joshua, and she intended taking the others that would make her a free woman. She had paid enough for her spoilt selfishness five years ago, forced to marry a man who didn't love her, losing her beloved Lindy; her love for Joshua was dead too now.

The dinner party that evening was like hundreds of others she had attended since she had become Joshua's wife, and she was far from the defiant child she had been the first time Joshua had introduced her to his friends, her awkwardness then about her obvious pregnancy making her uncomfortable with the people who had known Joshua for years. She had been so much younger than them then, in her manner as well as in years, was obviously an indiscretion on Joshua's part that he felt he should atone for with marriage.

But gradually over the years she had been accepted into the close-knit group. Tina Mayor had made that easier for her as the two of them met to shop or to let Lindy play with Tina's two small boys. Those meetings, as Joshua had pointed out last night, had been few and far between since Lindy's death, the sight of Tina's two little boys growing up healthy and strong reminding her all too forcibly of her own loss.

But the children were always in bed long before their parents dined, and so Joanna accompanied Joshua that evening with an easy heart.

Tina looked her usual beautiful self, a tall redhead with grace and style rather than actual beauty; she and Patrick shared a very close and loving marriage. Another reason Joanna felt uncomfortable with the other woman now—her own marriage bore no resemblance to her friend's, the loving way that Tina spoke of Patrick making her more aware of the fact that Joshua, her own husband, was a stranger to her.

They should never have married, she knew that, and

she felt sure Joshua did too. Thank God she had never had any more children after Lindy was born, as Joshua had wanted her to.

He had wanted them to be a normal family, had told her he would like other children, but she had recoiled from such an idea, nervous of having any more children when Lindy had been born with such a fatal defect. Patrick, and Joshua, had assured her that there was no possibility of Lindy's illness being hereditary, that any other child she had would almost certainly be born healthy. Nevertheless, she had refused to even think about other chilren. Now she was glad that she had.

Joshua looked as dark and distinguished as ever, his black dinner suit emphasising the width of his shoulders, his tapered waist, powerful thighs and long legs. There was more grey at his temples than she could ever remember noticing before, adding to his distinction, although he always seemed unaware of the female attention his good looks attracted. And no wonder, when he had a mistress like Angela Hailey!.

'You look wonderful,' Tina greeted her warmly, drawing her into the room and taking her over to join a group of laughing people, Joshua lingering behind to talk to Patrick. 'Men!' Tina grimaced. 'No doubt they're talking about work again.'

'Probably,' she nodded, wishing this evening were over so that she could work out the rest of her life.

'You would think they'd talked enough earlier today,' Tina mused.

Joanna was frowning now; she hadn't even known Joshua had seen Patrick today. Joshua rarely discussed his day with her now, and he certainly hadn't done so today, barely talking to her at all on the drive over here.

'You'll let me give you a party?'

She blinked at Tina, having no idea how youthful she

looked in the chocolate brown knit dress, her high-
heeled sandals giving her the look of a delicate child
trying to look older than she was. 'Sorry?' she frowned.

'I'd like to give you and Joshua a party.'

'That's nice,' Joanna answered stiltedly, wondering if
she had missed part of this conversation. Why on earth
should Tina want to give Joshua and her a party?

'When are you actually leaving?'

'Er——' She hadn't missed part of the conversation,
she really didn't have any idea what Tina was talking
about! She and Joshua had no intention of going
anywhere. She knew she had a habit of drifting off
when people spoke to her, but she could have sworn she
hadn't done so this time.

'I don't suppose you've worked out all the fine details
yet,' Tina nodded understandingly. 'But it's so exciting,
isn't it?'

'Er—yes.' Joanna began searching the crowded room
for Joshua, feeling out of her depth with this
conversation, sure that Joshua would be able to throw
some light on at least part of what Tina was talking
about.

'Have you been to America before? Of course you
have,' Tina answered her own question. 'I remember
you told me you were in Florida for several weeks
before you married Joshua. Patrick isn't too keen on
flying, so America is definitely out for us,' her friend
grimaced. 'A whole year of touring the States!' she
added enviously. 'And you're sure to stay in all the best
places. It's going to be so exciting!' she repeated
eagerly.

It suddenly became clear to Joanna what her friend
was talking about, although not why. Several months
ago Joshua had received an offer from America to tour
the medical schools lecturing to students. The two of

hem hadn't even discussed it, Joshua merely putting he letter to one side. Surely he hadn't decided they vere to go without even discussing it with her? She ouldn't believe even Joshua would be that arrogant.

She caught sight of him across the room, talking with Simon Shield, the heart specialist, a man in his late ifties; the respect between the two men was mutual. oshua was a complete stranger amongst these people o the man she had met in Canada five years ago, a man vho would dare to assume anything, and as his wife she vould be expected to simply agree with anything he :hose to do.

Her mouth tightened angrily, her days of following vhere he led were over. She didn't want to go to America for a year, she had no intention of going.

'Excuse me,' she interrupted Tina with cool politeness. I just have to see Joshua for a few minutes before dinner.'

'Of course,' her friend agreed lightly. 'I'll talk to you ater.'

Joanna made her way over to Joshua's side, acknowledging her friends as she made slow progress through them, putting her arm through the crook of Joshua's as she smiled up at the other man. 'How lovely to see you again, Simon,' she greeted smoothly. 'I haven't seen Daphne,' she mentioned his wife, aware that Joshua had stiffened as soon as she touched him, her own smile more of a strain than usual.

'She's staying with her mother for a few days. I couldn't get away,' Simon shrugged. 'Still, I don't have to explain to you how busy we doctors are.'

'You certainly don't,' she agreed softly.

'But you won't have that for much longer,' Simon said cheerfully. 'A whole year of freedom! You'll be able to treat it as a second honeymoon,' he added

with a twinkle in his eyes. 'Fascinating country
America.'

'So I've heard,' Joanna agreed tightly.

'Well, I must go and circulate,' Simon smiled at them
both. 'Daphne will want a full report at the weekend.'

'Give her my love,' Joanna said vaguely.

'I will,' he nodded, and moved away to talk to
another of his colleagues.

The smile remained fixed on her red-painted lips, bu
her eyes were bleak. 'When did you intend telling me?
she bit out tautly.

Joshua shrugged, not making any pretence not to
know what she was talking about. 'We had agreed to
talk later,' he said distantly. 'I would have told you
then. I had no idea the news would circulate so
quickly.'

'Didn't you?' she said with bitter humour. 'Joshua
Radcliffe decides to take a year off to tour America and
you don't think people will be interested! You're very
naïve, Joshua.'

'If you want an argument, Joanna, wait until we get
home!' he rasped harshly.

Her eyes widened. An argument? But they hadn't
argued, not really argued, for months and months. 'I
don't want to argue with you, Joshua,' she told him
calmly. 'There's nothing to argue about. I have no
intention of going to America with you for a year.'

His mouth tightened, his eyes glazing over icily. 'As
usual you've jumped to conclusions,' he bit out coldly.

'What do you mean?' Joanna asked slowly.

He glanced about them impatiently. 'I have no
intention of discussing this with you here.'

'But——'

'Not now, Joanna!'

She instantly fell silent. Joshua never raised his voice

:o her—he never needed to, a look was usually
sufficient. But he had shouted at her just now, evidence
of his own agitation. Joshua was a very controlled man,
always in command of himself and others, but he was
definitely disconcerted at the moment.

The rest of the evening passed in an agony of waiting
for Joanna, waiting to find out just what conclusion she
had jumped to. Either Joshua had made arrangements
for them to go to America or he hadn't. And it seemed
that he had.

'Patrick is absolutely thrilled that Joshua has asked
him to take over for him while you're away,' Tina
confided after dinner. 'And honoured too,' she laughed.
'Not many people could follow in Joshua's footsteps.'

Joanna smiled. 'I'm sure Patrick is going to be very
successful.'

Her friend frowned. 'You don't seem too thrilled
about America. I'd love it!'

'Simon thinks Joshua and I are taking a second
honeymoon,' Joanna told her friend dryly, not actually
making any comment about her feelings on going to the
States.

'Hardly, with the three of you going,' Tina derided.

Three of them? Heavens, not Angela Hailey? Surely
Joshua wasn't expecting her to spend a year in America
with him and his mistress? She had a feeling she knew
only too well who would be the unwanted third person,
and it wouldn't be Angela. She definitely wasn't going
under those circumstances!

She and Joshua went straight to the lounge when
they got home, Joshua tersely dismissing the housekeeper for the night when she came to check if they
wanted anything.

He took off his evening jacket, loosening the black
velvet bow tie he wore with the white silk shirt, moving

to pour himself a drink. 'Would you like one?' he enquired after his first swallow of whisky.

'No, thank you.' Joanna watched him coolly as he poured himself a refill before sitting in the chair opposite her.

He seemed in no hurry to begin talking, sitting back with his eyes closed, the lines of weariness about his nose and mouth more noticeable without the vitality of his eyes to alleviate his tiredness.

Suddenly the lashes flickered and he looked at her with cold grey eyes. 'We can talk now,' he stated flatly.

'Thank you!' Her sarcasm was barely contained. 'But I believe you're the one who has something to say.'

He sighed, the glass of whisky held loosely in his left hand, a plain gold wedding ring on the third finger of that hand. He looked down at the ring for several minutes, frowning darkly. 'I hadn't intended you to find out about the tour in the way you did,' he spoke softly, putting the glass in his other hand, dropping the left one down so that he no longer looked at the ring he wore. 'I was going to tell you about it now, explain to you——'

'*Tell* me?' she interrupted tautly. 'It's usual for a husband and wife to discuss things first, for them to decide *together* what their future should be!'

'You've already told me what yours is going to be.'

She frowned warily. 'I have?'

He nodded arrogantly. 'You said you aren't coming to the States with me.'

Joanna swallowed hard, unnerved by the calm way he seemed to be taking this, *accepting* it.

He stood up with forceful movements, as if the inactivity irked him. 'But I never intended that you should come with me,' he told her bluntly.

Her eyes widened, her hands clenching together in her lap. 'You—you didn't?'

'No,' he shook his head, not looking at her. 'This last year, since Lindy died, our marriage has become non-existent,' he continued flatly. 'I thought you needed time, to—adjust. And so I gave you time—and you just grew farther away from me than ever.'

She moistened her dry lips, aware that this conversation wasn't at all as she had envisaged it. It sounded as if *Joshua* was leaving *her*!

'The offer from the States was there, and I felt we needed to be away from each other for a while.'

'This last year——'

'We've continued to live together,' he said grimly. 'And it's been a disaster.' He sighed deeply. 'You can't be separated and still live in the same house, it just doesn't work.'

'No,' she agreed huskily. 'So that's what we're doing, separating?'

Joshua looked down at her with narrowed eyes. 'It's what you want, isn't it?' he rasped.

'Yes.'

He nodded abruptly. 'It's what I feel we should do too.'

It had all been so much easier than she had thought. For all that they had drifted apart this past year she hadn't expected Joshua to be quite so amenable about their divorce. It left her with a feeling of anti-climax.

'—and see how we both feel then,' Joshua concluded.

Joanna blinked, frowning her consternation. 'Sorry?' she said uncertainly, so deep in thought she had missed the rest of what he was saying.

'Joanna, this would be so much easier if you would just listen,' he snapped impatiently. 'I'm proposing a year's separation, completely no contact with each other, and then after that time, when my contract in the

States is up, seeing how we both feel about our marriage.'

'But I thought—We aren't getting a divorce?'

His mouth tightened. 'No.'

'Why aren't we?' she frowned.

'Because it's too damned easy, that's why!' he bit out furiously, his eyes stormy. 'Any kind of severing of a relationship is too easy nowadays.'

'But we never had any real relationship,' she protested. 'We were married because of Lindy, and now she—she's—there's no need to go on with the marriage any more now she's gone.'

'What's one more year out of your life, Joanna?' he asked coldly.

'You've already had five!' Tears glistened in her deep blue eyes.

He seemed to pale, a nerve beating erratically in his cheek. 'And in another year you'll still only be twenty-four. Give me one more year, Joanna.'

'No . . .' she shook her head.

'Please!'

She swallowed hard, never having known him plead for anything before. 'What good would it do?' she sighed. 'Nothing will have changed in a year.'

'I'm hoping we both will have.'

'But the *situation* won't! I'll still be married to you and wishing I weren't, and you'll still be married to me and wishing you weren't. I know you're taking Angela with you, Joshua,' she told him softly. 'Am I supposed to sit here in London waiting faithfully for my husband to come back from a year spent with his mistress?' she scorned.

'No,' he rasped. 'You're supposed to go out and find *yourself* a lover for a year!'

'What?' she gasped weakly.

'We'll be totally separated, Joanna,' he informed her harshly. 'Live our own lives, have our own friends. You, and I, will be totally free to be with whom we like, sleep with whom we like, for that year.'

CHAPTER FIVE

SHE stared at him incredulously, going to speak several times, but unable to get the words out. She hadn't even guessed Joshua meant to come out with such a plan, had had no warning, and was consequently speechless.

'Well?' he finally prompted harshly.

'We might as well be divorced,' she frowned.

'No,' he bit out. 'This way we have another chance.'

'How many do we need?' she derided.

Joshua's mouth tightened at her sarcasm. 'We don't need any, we're *giving* ourselves this one.'

'But what's the point?'

'The point is that we're *married*,' he rasped. 'The vows I made to you five years ago meant something to me then and they mean something to me now. If after this year away from each other you've made a separate life for yourself, don't—don't need me any more, then I'll give you your divorce.'

'And if I won't agree to the year?'

'Then you'll have to wait two years to divorce me, because I'll never agree to it now!'

She searched the harshness of his face, knew by the icy fire in his eyes, his flared nostrils, the uncompromising tightness of his mouth, that he meant it. Another *two years* tied to this man? She couldn't stand it!

'What are the arrangements?' she asked dully.

His mouth twisted mockingly at her capitulation. 'I thought you might see reason once I'd explained the circumstances to you.' He moved to pour himself another drink. 'Are you sure I can't get you something?'

86

'Whisky,' she requested abruptly. 'Neat.'

He ignored the latter request, adding a liberal amount of water plus ice to her drink. 'We may as well both be sober while we discuss this separation,' he smiled tightly, handing her the glass before sitting opposite her.

He was so supremely confident, always had been, and Joanna had never quite lost that feeling of being a child when she was with him. Which was ridiculous in the circumstances—she had been a wife and mother for five years!

'I suggest you stay here in the house——'

'No,' she instantly refused.

He looked at her warily. 'No?'

She shook her head. 'You said—you said we would live our own lives, have our own—friends. I could hardly bring any men back here,' she derided.

Joshua nodded, swallowing some of his whisky. 'Point taken. You'll take a flat in town?'

How could he discuss the idea of her having other men if there was a vestige of feeling for her in his heart? She didn't think he could. The fact that he intended spending the next year with Angela Hailey filled her with disgust rather than any other emotion, evidence of her own lack of love for him. But how did he really feel about the possibility of her having other men during his absence, how could he feel when he discussed it so unemotionally?

'Joshua——'

'I've seen some rather nice ones in Hampstead. Perhaps we could go and look at them before I leave?'

'I'll go on my own,' she told him firmly. 'And I'll choose my home on my own. Hampstead is too near my moth—my parents,' she amended with a blush.

'Very well,' Joshua agreed distantly.

Joanna's brows rose at his easy acceptance of her stubbornness over her future home. She had become so accustomed to Joshua making the decisions in their marriage that the thought of having a year of freedom, of doing what she wanted, living where she wanted, filled her with elation.

'When do you leave?' she asked now.

His mouth twisted with wry humour. 'Can't wait to see me go, hmm?' he mocked.

She gave a shrug of nonchalance. 'I imagined you couldn't wait to get away. I'm sure Angela is—very eager.'

'Angela is going as my secretary, Joanna,' he told her tautly.

'That isn't an original name for it,' she derided.

His mouth tightened as she mocked him. Joshua wasn't a man that you dared scorn, not if you wanted to escape unscathed. She had been stupid and naïve not to have seen the hard ruthlessness in him when they had met five years ago.

'It will be her official title nonetheless,' he rasped abruptly.

She raised blonde brows. 'And her unofficial one?'

'Joanna——'

'You don't deny that you're having an affair with her, do you, Joshua?' she scorned. 'Just how long *has* it been going on?' she queried lightly.

'I really don't see why——'

'I need to know?' she finished with sarcasm. 'Don't they say the wife is always the last to know? I just want to know how long people have been gossiping about my husband and his secretary.'

'I haven't been aware that any one has,' he said with arrogance.

'Of course you haven't,' she snapped. 'They gossip

about you, not *to* you. How long have you been seeing Angela away from work?'

He seemed to hesitate, his eyes a cold grey, then he nodded, shrugging. 'I've slept with Angela for six months,' he stated distantly.

Joanna didn't know why she was stunned by this admission, she had always known Joshua was a highly sensual man, that until Lindy died they had known a very physical marriage. It had been almost a year since she had denied him access to her bed and her body, and to his credit he had remained faithful for six months of that time.

'That means it's probably been public knowledge for at least five months of that time,' she told him stiffly.

'We've been very discreet——'

'That doesn't matter,' she shook her head. 'Someone always finds out.'

'Perhaps,' he acknowledged distantly. 'And to get back to your original question, I leave in six weeks. Can you stand to have me about for that long?' he mocked hardly.

'I think so,' she answered coldly. 'Although I would prefer it if we could keep to ourselves the fact that I won't be leaving with you for the moment.'

'Why?' His eyes were narrowed.

She sighed. 'I'm really not in the mood for one of my mother's lectures at the moment. I certainly couldn't stand six weeks of them!'

'No,' he ackowledged derisively. 'Neither could I. Very well, Joanna,' he stood up, 'for now we keep our separation to ourselves. Although I insist that your parents be told before I leave.'

'Why?'

'Because I want them to realise it was a joint decision,' he said curtly. 'Your mother hasn't always been kind to you in the past.'

'You noticed!'

'Don't be flippant, Joanna,' he dismissed harshly. 'I just don't want anyone to get the idea that either of us is in the wrong; we just need a breathing space from each other, time to know what we really want. I want your parents to understand that.'

Joanna was grateful for his thoughtfulness. Since the time she had 'let down' her parents—her mother's words, not her own—by becoming pregnant before she was married, it had been an uphill effort for her to do anything right in their eyes. In the end she didn't even try any more; her mother's criticism had been very biting, her praise of Joshua unshakeable. If her mother believed she had wanted this separation from Joshua, that she had asked for it, her life wouldn't be worth living.

As it was, her mother was very voluble in her disapproval of Joshua going to America without Joanna. Joshua had decided the week before his departure that her parents should be told the truth, and during that last Sunday lunch with them he told them. They both showed stunned surprise, although neither probed too deeply at the time, seeming to accept that it was their decision and their decision alone.

When Joanna met her mother for lunch the next day it was a different matter!

'Are you mad, Joanna?' she demanded heatedly. 'A year's separation from a man like Joshua could turn into a permanent one!'

'It's his decision,' Joanna shrugged.

'One I'm sure you could have talked him out of if you'd wanted to,' her mother insisted waspishly.

'Maybe I didn't want to.'

'It isn't because of your writing, is it?' she frowned. 'I've heard Joshua say nothing but praise about this new career you've found for yourself. Besides, you can write anywhere, you don't have to stay in London for it.'

Joanna had seen James Colnbrook several times during the last few weeks, had signed a contract with him to do several more books, had also had it arranged for her to meet Dan Cameron, the man who was to illustrate the first book, and the others too once she had written them. Everything seemed to be running smoothly in that direction, even the second 'Billy' book was starting to take shape in her mind.

'Joshua doesn't want me to go with him, Mother, it was his suggestion that he go alone.'

'Taking Angela Hailey isn't exactly going alone!' her mother derided cuttingly.

'No, but there's a difference—he *wants* Angela with him.'

'I can't believe you're taking this so calmly, Joanna,' her mother gasped. 'I really think you're making a mistake.'

'That's my prerogative.'

'Don't be foolish, Joanna! And this business of moving into your own flat——'

'Is *my* business,' she cut in abruptly. 'Joshua has seen it, and he approves.' Despite misgivings she had finally agreed to show Joshua her flat, expecting him to criticise its smallness, to be angry at her decision to live alone without servants. He had said nothing.

Her mother gave an impatient sigh. 'The two of you are behaving ridiculously!'

'Do you think so?' she mused. 'I thought we were acting very maturely. And we aren't the first couple to try a trial separation.'

'I realise that,' her mother snapped. 'But these trial separations often become a permanent arrangement.'

Joanna shrugged. 'I'm sure that in those cases it's the best thing for everyone concerned.'

'If Lindy were alive there would be no question of separation!'

She paled at the mention of her daughter, looking at her mother with cold eyes. 'But Lindy isn't alive,' she rasped. 'And Joshua and I are both old enough to make our own decisions.'

'But——'

'I don't wish to discuss it any further, Mother.' She looked at her with steely eyes.

Her mother's mouth set in frustrated anger, but no more criticism was forthcoming for the moment.

Joanna met Dan Cameron for the first time later in the week, instantly liking the tall redhaired Scot, finding his biting humour amusing, his wicked mockery of James Colbrook's seriousness as he introduced them proving to be hilarious. James had left them shortly after the initial introduction, claiming a prior engagement, and Joanna looked around the untidiness of Dan's studio with interest.

'I read the book, by the way.' He followed her about the room as she looked at the sketches pinned to the walls with coloured studs.

While she was being introduced to Dan, a man of about thirty, she would guess, she had compared him to Joshua, as she had every other man she had met the last five years, and found him to be the exact opposite in everything to her husband. His copper-coloured hair was worn long and untidy, nothing like Joshua's neat style, Dan's face full of humour, laughter lines beside his eyes and mouth, Joshua's normal expression one of austerity, Dan's way of dressing casual, a ragged teeshirt and faded denims, even Joshua's casual clothing superbly tailored.

She liked Dan on sight, and she turned to smile at him shyly now. 'You did?' she grimaced. 'I—What did you think of it? No, strike that question,' she frowned. 'That was unfair of me.'

'I liked it,' he told her cheerfully. 'Billy reminded me of a dog I had when I was a kid.'

'Me too! I mean—he *was* a dog I had when I was a child,' she blushed.

'I guessed that,' he nodded. 'Do you happen to have a photograph of him?'

Joanna frowned. 'Why?' she asked in a puzzled voice.

'You have the final okay on any illustrations I do, right?'

Joshua had taken an interest in the contract she was to sign with the publishing company, and had taken it to a lawyer to be checked over first. The stipulation about the illustrations had been only one of the changes the lawyer had advised. When Joanna had seen some of the others she had wondered if perhaps Joshua was trying to lose her the contract, sure that James Colnbrook couldn't agree to any of them. He had agreed to them all.

'Yes,' she confirmed, still puzzled.

'And it could take me days just to find the right sort of format for Billy, let alone the other characters in the book. If I could have a photograph of the original dog I'm sure I could come up with exactly what you want.' He grinned in triumph at his reasoning.

'Very clever,' she drawled, opening her clutch-bag to take out her wallet. 'I only have this one of him, so don't lose it,' she warned as she searched through the contents of her wallet.

Dan held up his hands defensively, his brown eyes warm. 'I'll guard it with my life,' he promised teasingly.

At the time that she had Billy Joanna hadn't had a camera of her own, and quite by chance her mother had taken a photograph of him as he played in the garden with a ball. The photograph was primarily of Joanna, but as soon as her mother had seen Billy was in the background she had thrown it away in disgust. Joanna had retrieved it from the bin as soon as she could, and it had stayed with her ever since, cut down to size, her own girlish figure no longer there as she shaped it to fit in her wallet.

'Ah, here we are.' She pulled out the slightly faded photograph, dropping several others on the floor in the process. 'Damn!' She bent down to pick them up.

So did Dan Cameron, and the two of them bumped heads. He looked at her with pained eyes, rubbing his forehead. 'I didn't realise it was dark enough for stars!' He blinked to clear his head.

Joanna laughed lightly, massaging her own bruised forehead, feeling a slight lump there already.

Dan's humour faded, his eyes taking on a deep glow as he looked at her. 'You're really quite beautiful when you laugh,' he said huskily.

She stiffened, her own humour fading; she was unused to such compliments, knowing he was flirting with her. 'Thank you,' she said abruptly. 'Now would you mind helping me with these?' She got down on the floor to pick up the scattered photographs.

He came down on his knees beside her, looking at each photograph as he picked it up.

'They're private,' she snapped, glaring at him.

His brows rose at her vehemence. 'I was only looking——'

'Well, don't!' She snatched the photographs out of his hand, one of them fluttering down again in her haste to put them away.

Dan instantly picked it up, looking down at the little girl shown there, her dark hair curling round her face, her eyes huge in her thin face, although the smile on her lips did a lot to alleviate her look of illness. 'Pretty,' Dan murmured thoughtfully. 'She has a look of you about her—Hey!' he protested softly as she snatched this photograph away more vehemently than the others. 'I was only saying——'

'She's my daughter—Lindy.' Joanna stood up, her agitation making her movements jerky.

'James told me you're married,' Dan nodded. 'He didn't say anything about children, though.'

'That's because there aren't any now.' Her voice was brittle. 'And there won't be a husband either after tomorrow.'

The brown eyes darkened with puzzlement. 'You're leaving your husband?' he questioned slowly.

She gave a derisive laugh. '*He* is leaving *me*,' she corrected. 'I'm sorry,' she sighed, ruffling her blonde hair with a shaking hand. 'I shouldn't be bothering you with this, we've only just met.'

'Sometimes it's easier to talk then,' he prompted softly.

She shook her head. 'Not for me. Maybe I'll tell you about it one day,' she forced a smile to her stiff lips. 'If I know you long enough.'

'Oh, you will,' Dan nodded confidently. 'The *Billy* books are going to be as popular as Paddington Bear!'

'Says you as a critic!' she teased, angry with herself for letting her cool reserve slip in that way.

'Says me as the man who has to sit here day after day illustrating kids' books,' he corrected dryly. 'You'll be around for a long time to come, Joanna Radcliffe.'

'I'll see you next week—Dan Cameron,' she returned lightly, handing him the requested picture of Billy.

The two of them had agreed to meet once a week to monitor Dan's progress—or lack of it. Although he assured her his illustrations would be fantastic! Strangely enough she believed him.

Dan was unlike any other man she had ever met. Most of Joshua's friends tended to be on the serious side, while her own male friends amounted to nil. Find yourself a lover, Joshua had told her—but how was she supposed to do that when she didn't even know any men? Her eyes widened as she looked at Dan.

He glanced up from looking at the picture of Billy, his eyes narrowing. 'What are you looking at me like that for?' he asked bluntly.

Hot colour flooded her cheeks, and James Colnbrook would have been very surprised to see how his cool new author could blush so shyly. 'I—er—I like your teeshirt,' she invented lamely.

He grinned. '"I AM A SEX OBJECT",' he read. 'I can get you one like it if you want,' accepting this as the reason she had been staring at him.

'Er—no, thanks.' She could just imagine Joshua's reaction to her wearing something like that! But Joshua wouldn't be here to see what she wore after tomorrow. 'I'll be shopping myself on Monday, maybe I'll get one then.' She smiled to herself at the thought of wearing the casual clothes Dan favoured. Things were certainly going to be different for her the next year!

Dan nodded. 'And I'll see you on Wednesday. I'll look forward to it,' he added throatily.

So was she, strangely enough. Surely she wasn't taking seriously that ridiculous notion she had in Dan's studio? He was attractive enough, very charming too, but just because Joshua had 'given his permission' to her finding herself a lover it didn't mean she had to do just that. This year without a man trying to control her life was going to be heaven, she didn't intend complicating it with another man, not now, and not for a few years to come either.

She hummed softly to herself on the drive over to her parents' house that evening, her mother insisting that any farewell party for Joshua would be given at her house and not at Tina's.

'You seem happy tonight.' Joshua glanced over at her in the darkness as he drove them himself.

'I am,' she nodded.

Joshua had been his usual self the last six weeks, perhaps spending a little more time than usual at the clinic, although he claimed that this was due to the fact that he wanted to leave everything in order for Patrick to take over from him. Joanna didn't dispute that, although she had a feeling Angela Hailey might have had something to do with a few of those late evenings.

'You're that glad to be rid of me?' There was a steely edge to his voice.

It wasn't that she wanted to be rid of Joshua, or that she actually hated him, she knew that now; she just needed to be away from him, to be by herself, to *find* herself. Joshua wasn't to blame for the failure of their marriage, she was, and she wanted him now to have whatever was going to make him happy. Angela Hailey seemed to be that.

'Isn't the feeling mutual?' she said lightly.

He drew in a ragged breath, his hands momentarily tightening on the steering-wheel. 'It's for the best,' he nodded. 'How did the meeting with the illustrator go today?'

Joshua had shown a great deal of interest in her new career, and she had enjoyed disussing it with him the last few weeks. She was going to miss that, at least.

'Dan seems very nice,' she told him. 'And he likes the book.'

'So did I.' His praise wasn't in the least patronising, and she knew he had been genuinely surprised and proud of her work.

He had asked to read the carbon copy of her book several weeks ago, and after protesting loudly at first Joanna had finally allowed him to see it, cringing with embarrassment most of the time he read it, pretending to be busy with a tapestry she was working on, all the time shooting his unrevealing face anxious looks as he said nothing.

Finally he had put the last typewritten sheet down, turning to look at her with eyes glowing with pride and appreciation. The words of praise had been unnecessary after that look, but Joshua had said them anyway.

'I know you did,' she said now. 'But Dan sees hundreds of them, and he still liked it.'

Joshua's mouth tightened, his expression grim. 'I see,' he bit out tautly. 'Then let's hope he knows what he's talking about!'

Her happy mood suddenly faded at his sneering attitude, and she felt something inside her shrivel up and die, accepting once again that she and Joshua couldn't even communicate on a level of politeness. Oh, they tried, they had really tried this last six weeks, and with a few cutting words Joshua had once again demoralised her. She didn't need his damned approval anyway, she thought bitterly. He would be gone tomorrow, and then she wouldn't have to take any more of his disapproving, moralising attitude.

'Let's at least try and give the impression we're still happy together.' He helped her out of the car when they arrived at her parents' house.

'Why bother?' she sighed. 'It will be all over London

in a few days that I haven't gone with you.' She smoothed down her long blue velvet dress.

His mouth tightened. 'For your mother's sake let's just put on a show for this one last night. It will mean a lot to her.' He looked magnificent in his black evening suit.

Joanna wanted to know when he had suddenly become so concerned about pleasing her mother, but she could only nod in agreement, the frightened child who had become his wife still not erased as she weakly allowed him to take control, his arm about her waist as they entered the house of laughing, excitable people.

Joshua was the loving, attentive husband all evening, so much so that her mother wondered if she weren't going to America after all.

'I still think you're a fool,' her mother rasped when told that wasn't the case. 'You'll lose him completely.'

'I'll bear your advice in mind at the divorce, Mother,' Joanna answered dryly.

'There's never been a divorce in our family!'

Her mouth twisted. 'It happens in the best of them, Mother,' she drawled derisively.

'Oh dear, I don't know you like this, Joanna,' her mother sighed. 'You're like a stranger.'

'That isn't surprising,' she said tightly. 'I am a stranger, to both you and Daddy. I made a mistake in my life, but I don't intend to continue suffering for that mistake any more.'

'I thought you said it was a trial separation?' her mother said sharply.

Joanna blushed, looking away, knowing that she could be separated from Joshua for *ten* years and still know now that she wanted a divorce. 'I'm sure you remember your own answer to that,' she told her mother stiffly, and moved away.

In actual fact no one looking at either herself or Joshua could have guessed that they meant to part the next day; they were more natural with each other tonight than they had been in a long time. Joanna's mood was so mellow by the time they drove home that she thought nothing of Joshua's request that they have a nightcap together in the lounge, where a fire was burning in the hearth.

'I've arranged for Mrs Barnaby to continue to keep the house prepared for our use,' he handed her the glass of white wine she had asked for, sitting next to her on the sofa. 'So if you would like to come back here at any time——'

'I don't envisage that happening,' she shook her head, her hair very blonde against the dark material of her dress.

'No, possibly not,' he agreed distantly. 'I know you've preferred not to discuss these things, Joanna, but I just want you to know that everything has been taken care of while I'm away. The bills will be paid by the bank, the——'

'I'm not really interested, Joshua,' she told him huskily. 'Not just now.' For the first time in months she could feel his physical pull on her, could feel her senses leap at how darkly attractive he was, how strong and capable his hands, hands that knew how to caress her to mindless pleasure, the lean strength of his body just as versed in showing that pleasure!

The eroticism of her thoughts made her turn away in confusion. She hadn't thought of Joshua in this physical way for months, had remembered only his arrogance and coldness, his ruthlessness when it came to something he wanted. But she thought of him now, of all the nights they had given themselves to each other, of the burning caresses that reduced her bones to jelly, of the way Joshua's lips and tongue knew every inch of her body, of how he was leaving her tomorrow . . .

'Joanna?' Joshua was frowning at her bent head, although a fire blazed deep in his eyes as she looked up and he could see the languorous longing in her eyes. 'Joanna!' he rasped, putting his glass down to take hers out of her hand and place it next to his own on the coffee table. 'Darling . . .?' he questioned, his hands on her shoulders bringing her hard against him.

She swallowed hard, not at all sure what was happening to her, the ache in her body deepening until it was almost a pain.

Her eyes widened as Joshua's mouth came down gently on hers, the movement of lips against lips slow and questioning, probing the edge of her teeth, smoothly searching out almost-forgotten pleasures as she allowed him access to the deep warmth of her mouth.

There was none of her usual panic at having him this close to her, and as his mouth travelled slowly to her ear, biting on the lobe, she gave a low groan in her throat, her arms moving up his chest and over his shoulders as she hungrily caressed the dark hair at his nape.

Joshua moaned as she caressed his chest beneath his shirt, her avid fingers having unbuttoned it down to his navel, loving the feel of the silky hair that covered most of his body. 'Joanna——'

'No, don't talk,' she put silencing fingertips to his lips. 'I don't want to talk any more tonight, it's too late for that.'

'But——'

'Just let our bodies do the talking.' She took his hand and placed it on her breast, her nipple tautening at the unaccustomed feel of his thumbtip moving against the sensitive flesh. 'That's right,' she gasped as her excitement grew. 'Oh, Joshua,' she groaned as the ache in her body grew into a flame. 'You always did know how to arouse me!' Her eyes were closed as he slid the zip of her dress down her spine, pushing the material down to her waist, her breasts now bared to his questing tongue and teeth, a fact he took full advantage of.

His lips roamed sensuously around the taut peak of her breast, soft and warm as they encountered the hardened nipple, the gentle nip of his teeth causing her to shudder with pleasure.

When he stood up she felt bereft, holding out her arms to him in silent pleading, not caring in that moment that he was leaving her tomorrow, that he had a mistress, a woman who had shared this warmth with him for the last six months. She wanted him, *needed* him, he couldn't leave her now!

He threw off his jacket and bow tie, leaving his shirt loose as he moved to close the door, turning the key in the lock, extinguishing the lights so that only the warm glow of the fire lit his way back to her. He pulled her effortlessly to her feet in front of him, sliding the dress the rest of the way down her body, only her lace panties covering her nakedness now.

Joshua's breath seemed to catch in his throat as he looked down at her, at her proudly thrusting breasts, her tautly flat stomach, the mound of her womanhood soft against the silky blue panties, her legs long and shapely, her shoes kicked off long ago. 'You're the most exciting woman I've ever seen,' he told her gruffly, his hand trembling slightly as it moved over the soft invitation of her breast, fingers touching delicately as they moved to take off her last piece of clothing.

Joanna's hands weren't idle either, removing his shirt

from widely muscled shoulders, her lips caressing the salty hardness of his chest, feeling his indrawn breath as she slowly unzipped his trousers to remove them completely, her position on her knees in front of him subservient to an onlooker, but she knew that she was the one in control as she began to kiss him, his rasped shuddering breaths telling her that he was almost at the end of his endurance of such intimate kisses.

He fell to his knees beside her in front of the fire, the scene so poignant of another memorable one that with a choked cry she joined her body with his, instantly feeling the spasms of pleasure shoot through his body, knowing that the release she was already experiencing wasn't far off for Joshua either, that their desire for each other had been denied for so long it was rocketing out of contol, and taking them with it.

With a final groan of aching desire Joshua took her into the whirlpool of sensual delight, the two of them clinging to each other as they were tossed and torn in the desire of their making, their breathing ragged as the storm slowly quietened.

It had been so long for Joanna since she had known that true wonder, so long since her body had found that release in true satiation, that within seconds she had fallen asleep in Joshua's arms, feeling secure there, safe.

It was the unfamiliarity of a male body in the bed beside her that woke her later in the night, Joshua's hand possessive on her breast, tightening as he felt her move.

She turned in the haven of his arms, those same arms that had carried her up the stairs some time in the night. His dark hair was tousled from sleep, his eyes luminous as he opened heavy lids to look at her. What he saw in her face obviously satisfied him, as with a growl of intent he captured her mouth with his.

This time the loving was slow, their need not so intense, although their passion was. They rediscovered all the pleasure spots their haste the previous evening hadn't allowed for, and by the time Joshua's thrusting body finally claimed hers she was already bathed in a glow of sensual satisfaction.

She cradled him to her this time as he fell asleep, knowing they had reopened a closeness between them that would bind them together in spite of their other differences. Those other differences had never seemed to matter in the past, not when they could be close like this.

She slept with a feeling of well-being for the first time in months, her last thoughts ones of how she could possibly be ready to leave with Joshua for America in the morning. She would manage it somehow.

But there was no need to manage anything the next morning. It was after ten when she finally woke up, and Joshua had already left—with Angela.

CHAPTER SIX

'COME on, cheer up,' Dan encouraged. 'How am I supposed to sketch you when you look so miserable?'

Joanna sighed, making an effort to look more relaxed, although in reality she was as tense as a coiled spring. 'You aren't supposed to be sketching me at all,' she told him irritably. 'We're supposed to be completing the fourth *Billy* book.'

'All in good time,' he soothed. 'All in good time. And didn't I tell you how popular the *Billy* books were going to be?' he added knowingly.

'Yes,' she acknowledged dryly.

She had become good friends with Dan the last year, had come to rely on his friendship a great deal, having somehow felt lost and betrayed after Joshua left so abruptly. She had thought—assumed, after the night they had just spent together, that Joshua would want to resume their marriage, to have her accompany him to the States after all. His departure without her had given her all the answer she needed.

It had been a long year since his departure, acknowledging to herself, and accepting, that she still loved him, that the idea of her taking a lover was ludicrous.

But if she hadn't taken his advice and found herself a lover she had grown in a lot of other ways. She had written another two *Billy* books that James Colnbrook had put through for publishing, had learnt to live alone, and *be* alone, in her flat, to surround herself with the things she liked and felt comfortable with, having had Dan's help with the decorating.

Dan had turned out to be as nice a man as she had thought he was, and after his first couple of passes had got him nowhere he had decided to just be her friend, helping her all he could in her new life, taking her out and introducing her to his friends, making them her friends. And over a bottle of wine in his flat one evening she had even told him about Lindy. He had been her true friend since that night, the quiet way he had listened and not attempted to probe even making her love him a little, although she wasn't in love with him.

About Joshua she told him nothing—not of their marriage, of that last night together, or of the fact that she still loved her husband. It had come as a shock to her to realise that she loved Joshua, that he was the only man she ever would love, that last night spent in his arms having banished for ever the wall she had put about her emotions the night Lindy died. She knew now that she had never hated Joshua, had only shut him and the love she felt for him out of her life, and the tumbling of her defences had once again left her vulnerable to hurt by him.

'I hate to say I told you so,' Dan teased her now. 'But I did. Of course my illustrations of Billy do a lot to help sales,' he added modestly, frowning over the sketch he was doing of her.

'Of course,' she mocked.

He was frowning directly at her now. 'It's you that's all wrong, not my sketch.'

'I might have known!' she derided, strolling over to look at the drawing, small and fragile-looking in the fitted black denims and tailored silk blouse, her hair grown into a longer feathered style.

If she really looked anything like the haunted woman in Dan's sketch then she was more than miserable! Even in the black and white of a pencil drawing Dan had managed to catch the rather hunted look in her eyes, the weary line of her mouth, the tenseness of her body. It was all there on the paper, and she knew she would only have to look in the mirror to see it reflected there too.

She handed the sheet of paper wordlessly back to Dan, thrusting her hands into her denims pockets as she turned away. 'It's just that it's been a year now, over a year, and Joshua still hasn't come back.'

'One week and two days over now,' Dan confirmed that he too had been counting. 'I hope you aren't expecting any miracles when he does get back,' he warned softly.

Joanna flushed. 'What do you mean?'

He shrugged. 'I haven't fooled myself that it's loyalty to me that hasn't made you accept more than one date with the same man,' he drawled.

Through her new career and going out with Dan Joanna had met several men who had asked her out, and while she found most of them pleasant they hadn't interested her enough to go out with them a second time. None of them had burning grey eyes and a harshly beautiful face, none of them was Joshua.

'It could have been,' she told Dan lightly.

'No,' he shook his head firmly. 'I'm not stupid, Joanna, I know you still love your husband. The trouble is, *he* doesn't know that, and you aren't going to tell him, are you?'

'I don't even know where he is, Dan,' she scorned.

She had received only one communication from Joshua the last year, a huge bouquet of red roses on the day her first book was published, the card with them simply saying 'Congratulations, Joshua'. How he had known the publishing date she didn't know, and why he should choose to send the roses she daren't even guess. But the lovely blooms had been very welcome, and at least they had silenced her mother for a few weeks. But as the months passed and there was no further word from him her mother despaired.

Joanna despaired too, but she thought she had hidden it well. Obviously not well enough to fool Dan. That was the trouble with having friends, she had learnt this last year; they usually meant well, but some of their good intentions could turn out to be the opposite. Tina and Patrick had been very well intentioned since Joshua had left, often inviting her over to dinner, but treating her like a grass widow at the same time. In a way perhaps that was what she was, what she had *chosen* to be, but it was a little disconcerting to be treated that way.

'You wouldn't tell him even if you did,' Dan muttered now. 'You're a member of the so-called "élite society", Mrs Radcliffe,' he taunted. 'And words like love and fidelity aren't bandied about in your exclusive circle.'

She couldn't help smiling. 'That's snobbery in reverse, Mr Cameron,' she teased.

'Maybe so,' he accepted lightly. 'But it's the truth.'

'Tina and Patrick are happy and not afraid to show it,' she defended, having taken Dan to a party at her friends' house once. It had been an embarrassing as well as an awkward experience at first, but she had persisted in mixing her old friends with her new ones.

'Yes,' Dan acknowledged. 'But the majority of that crowd wouldn't know what love is if it hit them on the head. I don't know how you tolerate them, Joanna.'

She shrugged. 'They aren't that bad.'

His expression seemed to say otherwise, but he didn't

say any more. 'Is the party still on for tomorrow night?' he asked.

She grimaced, sighing heavily. 'It's going to be a waste of time without the guest of honour.'

Dan grinned. 'That's what happens when you forget to tell the man in question that you're giving a party for him!'

'I really thought he would be back by now,' she chewed on her bottom lip. 'It was to be a surprise for him.' And a way of showing Joshua that she was pleased at his return. Only he hadn't returned, hadn't given any indication that he intended doing so. 'I'm going over to the house now to see if Mrs Barnaby has heard anything from him.'

Dan looked up from his cross-legged position on the floor of her lounge. 'Is that a hint for me to leave?'

She laughed. 'How did you guess?'

'You're as subtle as a blow from a sledgehammer to the head!' He stood agilely to his feet. 'Why don't you just call the housekeeper?' He collected up the sketches and his pad that he had been working on this afternoon; the two of them often spent the day working together, sometimes at Dan's flat, sometimes at Joanna's.

She shrugged, turning away. 'It's more personal to go round. Besides, Joshua might actually be there, and then I——'

'Can see him for yourself,' Dan finished dryly. 'What's wrong, Joanna, don't you think he'll want to see you when he gets back?'

She flushed, chewing on the inside of her mouth. 'I—I don't know. He—I——'

'Hey, I'm sorry, Jo!' Dan put his arms around her, holding her close into his chest, using his pet name for her. 'I didn't mean to pry, your marriage is your affair.

I have to be going now anyway, or a tall leggy lady is going to be very disappointed,' he added with a suggestive leer.

His humour lightened her own tension, as it was designed to do, she felt sure, and she moved laughingly away from him. 'And we wouldn't want that, would we?' she teased.

'Not on your life!' he grinned, pulling on his lightweight bomber jacket. 'I'll bring Red to the party tomorrow, and then you can tell me what you think of her.'

'Red?' she questioned as she walked him to the door.

'She has glorious red hair right down to her——'

'Dan!'

He laughed softly, kissing her affectionately on the cheek. 'Well, she does. Her name is Carmella, by the way. And that's the only Italian thing about her. At least, I think it is,' he added wickedly.

'I'm sure you'll find out,' Joanna mocked gently as he left, his grin the only answer he gave her.

Her humour faded as soon as Dan had gone, and a pensive frown darkened her brow. She hadn't expected Joshua to return to England exactly a year to the day, but he was ten days overdue now, with no sign of his return.

The party at her flat, with their old friends and her new ones, had seemed a good idea at the time, a way, perhaps a gesture, of showing Joshua that her old and new life belonged together, that *they* belonged together. But Joshua's failure to appear had robbed the gesture of any meaning. Luckily most of the guests tomorrow would be unaware that the party had been given in his honour, the invitations she had sent out two weeks ago had been merely to a party, as she had decided at the time that the party would either be to show their friends they were reconciled or as a way of cheering her up if Joshua had decided they should divorce. The fact that he wouldn't have returned by this time hadn't occurred to her. Perhaps Mrs Barnaby would have heard something today.

'Nothing, Mrs Radcliffe,' the housekeeper told her with a sigh. 'I've had the house ready and the freezer stocked for the last month now, but there hasn't been so much as a telephone call from Mr Radcliffe.'

Joanna smiled through her disappointment. 'Never mind. He's probably just been delayed.'

'Probably.' The other woman looked quite dejected.

Joanna nodded. 'I'm just going upstairs for a moment, I—I have to get something from my room.' She turned towards the stairs.

'You'll be staying for dinner?'

'I——' Her refusal stopped in her throat as she saw the other woman's hopeful expression. If Mrs Barnaby were the sort of housekeeper who liked to be idle, who didn't enjoy every minute of running the household for them, the last year would have been wonderful for her. But Mrs Barnaby enjoyed every aspect of running this elegantly furnished house, and the last year had weighed heavily on her hands. 'That would be lovely, Mrs Barnaby,' she accepted warmly. 'One of your lovely apple pies for dessert?'

'Of course,' the housekeeper beamed. 'With fresh cream.'

'Delicious,' she smiled.

The housekeeper went back to her kitchen looking happier than she had in a long time. Mrs Barnaby had often tried to get her to stay to dinner in the past when she had called in at the house, and she had always refused until today. Maybe she was just delaying the time she would have to go back to her lonely flat, whatever her reason for accepting it had pleased Mrs Barnaby, and it also meant she wouldn't have to cook for herself this evening.

Her bedroom was as neat and clean as usual, but it was to Joshua's room she went. She had visited this room a lot the last year, had often just sat in the easy chair there and drunk in Joshua's presence, touched the bottles of cologne that stood on his dressing-table. It somehow brought the man himself closer to her.

'Mrs Radcliffe, I—Oh!' The housekeeper came to a halt in the open doorway as Joanna gave a guilty start at being caught in Joshua's bedroom. 'I—er—I was wondering if you would like a cup of tea or—or anything now?' Mrs Barnaby looked uncomfortable too.

'Yes—thank you.' The two bright wings of colour refused to fade from her cheeks. 'That would be nice,' Joanna added lamely.

As soon as the housekeeper had gone downstairs to get the tea she hastily left Joshua's room. It was bad enough that she should feel the need to moon about her husband's bedroom like a lovesick idiot, but to be caught doing it . . .!

How she came to be in Lindy's bedroom instead she never afterwards knew, but suddenly she was in the little pink and white bedroom, tears streaming down her face as she looked about the room that hadn't been changed since the day Lindy was taken out of it. Her daughter's rabbit lay on the made-up bed, the babyish drawings she had done pinned on the walls, the tiny furniture kept highly polished, the quilt on the bed patterned with kittens and puppies, a perfect match for the curtains at the windows.

It was all the way she had instructed it to be kept—and in that moment she knew it had to stop. Lindy was gone, there was no way she was ever going to come back to this pretty bedroom. After two years it was time to pack her things away, to give away what was no longer needed. And it was up to Joanna to do it.

She was sorting through the tiny clothes in the drawers when Mrs Barnaby came up with the tea-tray, and the housekeeper's gasp of surprise was met with a controlled smile, Joanna's tears dried now, her expression composed. 'Just leave the tray on the side.' She stood up, noticing how the other woman's hands shook as she put the tray down. 'I was just—just sorting through these old things,' Joanna told her lightly. 'I'm sure a hospital or perhaps a children's home would like some of the toys, a lot of them are practically new.'

Mrs Barnaby's mouth trembled emotionally. 'Oh, Mrs Radcliffe,' she choked. 'I don't—I've never——'

'I know.' Joanna put a comforting arm about the other woman's shoulders. 'We all loved Lindy, didn't we? But it's time to let her rest now. Do you have some boxes I could put these things into, something I can pack them away in?' she asked briskly before emotion threatened to overtake the housekeeper.

Mrs Barnaby controlled herself with an effort, nodding slowly. 'I'm sure I can find something. But are you sure——'

'Very,' she said firmly.

When she left the house three hours later she left with a sense of freedom, a feeling of putting the past well and truly behind her. She and Joshua might have married for their daughter's sake, but they would stay married for their own. She would fight Angela Hailey for Joshua—if it weren't already too late . . .

The party was going well, most of the guests being unaware that Joshua should have been here.

'Really, Joanna, did you have to invite that dreadful man?' Her mother glared across the room at Dan as he flirted with Daphne Shield, the older woman laughing coyly at something he had just said. 'He even tried to flirt with me earlier!' she added in a scandalised voice.

'He asked you to dance, Mother,' Joanna recalled dryly. 'That's hardly flirting.'

'The way he dances it is!'

She held back her laughter with effort. Dad had met her mother several times before tonight, and their dislike of each other was mutual. Dan took a fiendish delight in shocking her mother, and Joanna felt sure flirting with Daphne was just another way of doing that. He was a devil, and he was enjoying himself immensely, had winked at her mischievously only a couple of minutes ago.

'Where's Daddy?' she changed the subject.

'Over there somewhere,' her mother pointed vaguely across the room. 'Really, Joanna, this flat isn't big enough for all these people. And the music is much too loud,' she winced as yet another loud record was put on the stereo. 'Don't the neighbours complain?' she frowned.

Joanna laughed. 'Not when you invite them!' There were six other flats in the building, and she had taken care to invite all the occupants, a trick Dan had taught her. Luckily they had all come. 'Come on, Mother,' she encouraged lightly. 'Join in, have fun!'

'Joanna——'

'Excuse me, Mother,' she interrupted as she could see her mother was going to remain stubborn. 'I think I'd better save Daphne.'

'Someone had better!' her mother said with disgust.

Joanna shrugged off her mother's snobbish bad-humour, no longer so concerned with what her mother thought about anything. She put her hand through the crook of Dan's arm as she joined him and Daphne, although the older woman didn't look as if she needed rescuing. It seemed only her mother disapproved of her old and new friends mixing!

'It's a lovely party, Joanna,' Daphne told her.

'Thank you,' she smiled.

'When is Joshua—Why, here he is now!' Daphne exclaimed excitedly. 'What a lovely surprise, Joanna. We had no idea Joshua was coming back tonight!'

Neither had she! She was terrified to turn around to the doorway where Daphne was looking so enthusiastically. Joshua was here! But how——

'*That's* your husband?' Dan breathed softly.

Joanna swallowed hard, knowing she must have gone very white. She could just picture how Joshua would look, tall and attractive, looking every inch the successful man he was in one of those three-piece suits that fitted him so perfectly. No wonder Dan was so surprised—most people were when they realised such a distinguished man was her husband.

'Joanna.'

She stiffened at the sound of his husky voice behind her, and turned slowly, her eyes widening as she looked at a changed Joshua. No neatly styled short hair but an overlong windswept style that made him appear rakishly younger, and no three-piece suit either but a faded denim shirt that unbuttoned down his chest to reveal the dark hair that grew there, the cuffs turned back casually to the elbows, a pair of faded denims moulded tightly to the lean length of his legs, a pair of tan leather boots on his feet.

He wasn't the Joshua she remembered, and she could only stare at him wordlessly.

He stared right back at her, the grey eyes probing her

own appearance, making her conscious of the length of soft curly fair hair, the weight loss of the last year evident in her face and body, the latter made obvious by the clinging gold pants-suit she wore.

'Don't returning husbands get a welcome any more?'

Strangely it was Dan who asked the mocking question, and she knew he was challenging her to start doing something about getting her husband back. She gave him a furious glare before turning back to Joshua. Why shouldn't she welcome her husband home? Angela wasn't with him, and he was *her* husband.

'Darling!' she greeted huskily, going into his arms, raising herself on tiptoe to put her mouth against his, feeling him stiffen before he dropped the suitcase he was carrying to the floor, his arms going about her as he lifted her off the ground, his lips moving over hers hungrily, while the kiss went on and on.

'Maybe we should all just leave?' Dan's amused voice finally broke the spell, and other guests laughed softly.

Joshua raised his head, slowly lowering Joanna back to the carpeted floor, his arms dropping back to his sides. 'That won't be necessary,' he said smoothly; he was several inches taller than Dan, and he stood looking down at the other man with narrowed eyes. 'You must be Dan Cameron.'

'In the flesh,' Dan grinned, not at all disconcerted by being confronted by Joanna's husband like this. 'And I don't need any explanation as to who you are.'

'Joanna doesn't make a habit of kissing strangers at her parties?' Joshua drawled derisively.

'Not that I know of,' Dan answered cheerfully. 'And Jo's talked about you a lot.'

'Indeed?' Joshua said uninterestedly, turning back to Joanna. 'If you could show me the way to a bedroom I'll freshen up and join the party?' he prompted.

'I—Of course.' She had been in a state of shock since Joshua had entered her flat, surprised by his casual appearance, dumbfounded by the way he had responded to her attempt to kiss him. It had been just as if the last year had never happened, as if this were the day after they had made love so completely and Joshua was just returning home from work. 'Would you like to come this way?' she invited, automatically taking him to the spare bedroom, blushing as she realised she had done so. Well, she could hardly take him to her room, not until they had discussed what they were going to do!

She eyed him nervously as the door closed behind them, suddenly feeling very much alone with him despite the fifty or so other people in the flat.

He put the suitcase down on the bottom of the bed, then turned to look at her, very dark and virile. The longer hairstyle suited him, making him look more like the man she had first met in Canada. 'You're looking well,' he said softly.

'Thank you.' She laced her hands together in front of her, mainly to stop their shaking becoming noticeable. 'So—so are you,' she understated.

'Thanks.'

Not the greatest conversation in the world, they would be discussing the weather in a minute! 'Mrs Barnaby told you about the party?' Joanna asked brightly.

'No, I haven't been to the house.'

'Oh,' she frowned. 'You came straight here?'

'From the airport,' he nodded, sitting down on the single bed.

'Tired?' she prompted concernedly at the almost weary droop to his shoulders.

'A little,' he acknowledged softly.

'I—You're alone?' she queried nervously.

His mouth twisted. 'Yes, I'm alone. Your writing has been going well?'

'Yes—thank you.' God, they had to stop talking as if they were strangers! 'Thank you for the roses, they were beautiful.'

'The least I could do,' he shrugged dismissively.

'How did the tour go?'

'Very well.'

'Good.' Heavens, this was terrible, worse than she had ever imagined! 'I—er—I went to the house yesterday.'

His expression became wary, his eyes narrowed. 'Mrs Barnaby is well?'

'Missing have you there to look after.' She gave a light laugh to try and ease the tension she still felt. All she wanted to do was launch herself into his arms, tell him how much she loved him, and yet she couldn't move, couldn't tell him how she felt, she was too shy with him. 'I even stopped to dinner when I hadn't intended to.'

'I'm sure she liked that.'

'Yes. I—er——' she chewed her bottom lip, 'I sorted through Lindy's things while I was there. Mrs Barnaby is going to give most of them to charity.'

Joshua had stiffened at her mention of their daughter's name, his expression stony now, his eyes glacial. 'I see,' he said tautly.

'Unless there's something you would like to keep, of course,' she added hastily. 'I—I just thought it was time.'

'Yes,' he agreed abruptly, and stood up, suddenly making the room seem very small. 'You've seen a lot of Cameron while I've been away?' He arched dark brows over narrowed eyes.

'Quite a bit,' she nodded, feeling on safer ground

now, even managing to smile a little. 'The illustrations he's done for the books have been wonderful.'

'I've seen them.'

Her eyes widened to surprised blue pools. 'You have?'

'Of course,' his mouth twisted. 'Although it took me some time to realise that the reason I couldn't locate one of your books was because it was published under the name of J. Proctor.'

'I——' Joanna moistened her dry lips, wishing she could summon some of that cool sophistication that had been second nature to her a year ago. 'I thought it best,' she finally managed to say, loving this man so much she ached with it, longing to touch him, to reach out to him. But she couldn't, not when he showed no sign of wanting her to do any of those things.

'Why?'

She swallowed hard. 'I had no idea what your reaction would be to my using your name——'

'Your name too,' he put in abruptly. 'Unless you've done anything to change that while I've been in the States?' His eyes narrowed even more.

Joanna paled. 'I—No,' she shook her head. 'I thought we'd agreed to wait until you returned before making any decisions,' she watched him anxiously.

'Yes.' He ran a hand round the back of his neck. 'I had no idea I would be walking in on a party tonight, otherwise I——'

'Oh, but——'

'Jo!' a gentle knock sounded on the door, and Dan's voice was discernible to them through its thickness.

Joshua's mouth tightened before he strode across the room to open the door with forceful movements. 'Joanna is busy right now,' he rasped. 'Is there anything *I* can do for you?'

Dan looked up at the older man, obviously weighing up the situation, a mischievous smile lighting up his features. 'I don't think so, it was Jo I wanted. Sweetheart, your guests are starting to feel neglected.' He ignored her start of surprise his endearment caused, looking up at Joshua challengingly. 'I realise this is your first evening home, old man, but the party must go on and all that,' he mocked. 'Perhaps if we'd known of your return we could have——'

'Dan!' Joanna had finally found her voice, shocked at the misconception he was nurturing.

'Sorry, love.' Dan strolled into the room, putting his arm about her shoulders. 'But surely you can say your hellos to Josh later?'

'Joshua,' she corrected tautly, glaring up at him.

'Joshua,' he shrugged dismissively. 'You don't mind if I take Jo back to the party, do you?' he prompted the other man. 'It's all a bit flat without our beautiful hostess.'

'His beautiful hostess' could cheerfully have hit him at that moment, and if anything Joshua had become more remote than ever.

'You go ahead, Joanna,' he told her now. 'I'll join you later.'

She could hardly contain her anger until she and Dan were outside the bedroom, turning on him angrily once they were out in the hallway. 'What on earth did you think you were doing?' she snapped, her eyes glittering in her fury. 'You've given Joshua completely the wrong impression about us!'

Dan looked unrepentant. 'You started off well, that kiss looked pretty impressive, but I could see things had broken down a little since you were alone together. I could have cut the atmosphere with a knife just now.'

Her hands were clenched into fists at her sides. 'And

what good do you think your charade has done?' she demanded furiously.

'A little jealousy never hurt anyone,' he shrugged.

'Oh, Dan, how could you!' she groaned, her hands to her face. 'Joshua's going to think—well, you know what he's going to think!' she choked, the tears falling unbidden.

Dan took her into his arms. 'Don't worry, love, it isn't that bad. Look, if you're that worried about it,' he added as she continued to cry, 'I'll tell him the truth.'

'I don't think he cares,' she sobbed into his chest, remembering Joshua's lack of emotion as he said he would join them later.

'Of course he cares,' Dan scoffed. 'And don't worry, I'll take care of everything. Have I ever let you down yet?' he attempted to tease.

'Excuse me,' rasped a chilling voice. 'I'd like to get past to the bathroom.'

Joanna swallowed hard, turning to face her husband. 'Joshua——'

'This isn't the way it seems,' Dan blustered into speech. 'It's been a shock for Jo to see you like this, and I——'

'Please don't feel you have to explain yourself to me,' Joshua cut in coldly. 'As you said earlier, perhaps if you'd known of my return . . . Now I really would like to freshen up, it's been a long day.' He brushed past them and into the bathroom.

'God, I'm sorry, love,' Dan groaned at Joanna's stricken look. 'It was just—He wasn't what I was expecting at all. The way you described him, the things you told me about him,' he shook his head, 'I was expecting an aged man with a roving eye, not that handsome devil. No wonder the rest of us never stood a chance with you!'

A thin watery smile lightened Joanna's expression. Joshua's changed appearance had come as shock to her too, although he had never been Dan's first impression of him either. 'America obviously agreed with him,' she said stiltedly, wondering how much influence Angela Hailey had had on the changes in Joshua.

'Obviously,' Dan said dryly, leaning back against the wall, giving the impression he had every intention of staying there.

Joanna turned. 'Aren't you coming back to the party?' she frowned.

He grimaced. 'I think I should stay and explain to your husband that I was only kidding just now. Do you think he'll punch the hell out of me now or just challenge me to pistols at dawn?'

She laughed outright at his woebegone expression. 'Neither. But I might do the latter,' she added warningly.

'I was only trying to help,' he groaned. 'I thought maybe he just needed a little prodding in the right direction.' He pulled a face. 'He isn't a man who likes to be prodded, is he?'

'How did you guess?'

'Intuition, I suppose. A little late, but I catch on eventually,' he grimaced. 'Don't worry, love, I'll straighten everything out.'

'No,' she shook her head. 'Just leave it for now, Dan. This is a party, I can talk to Joshua when everyone has gone home.'

'Sure?' he frowned.

'Very,' she nodded, throwing an anxious look in the direction of the bathroom door. 'Yes, very sure.'

It would be better if she explained everything to Joshua herself, and maybe later tonight she could tell him that she loved him, that she didn't want their separation to continue but wanted to stay married to him.

'Go and talk to Carmella,' she encouraged Dan once they got back to the lounge. 'She looks neglected.' The tall willowy redhead was listening to one of Joshua's colleagues with a polite but bored smile on her face.

'Isn't she beautiful?' Dan followed her line of vision, a smile of anticipation on his lips.

'Very,' Joanna agreed dryly, wondering if this one would have brains as well as a beautiful face and body; Dan's women rarely had both intelligence and beauty. 'When are you going to find the right woman and settle down?'

'Never, I hope,' he grinned. 'Wish me luck, Jo. Carmella doesn't allow sex on the first date; today is our second one,' he added pointedly.

Her smile was indulgent. 'When are you ever going to grow up, Dan?'

'I am grown up,' he gave a suggestive leer. 'As Miss Carmella Nero is about to find out!'

Joanna watched as the willowy model entwined herself about Dan, the wink he gave Joanna one of triumph. If Joshua could see Dan and Carmella now there wouldn't be any confusion as to the direction Dan's interest took!

But Joshua was still in the bedroom changing, and Dan and Carmella left before he could come out and join the party, a smile of satisfaction on Dan's face.

'How wonderful that Joshua should arrive back tonight!' Her mother appeared at her side. 'Perhaps now you'll drop these unsuitable bohemian friends of yours and behave like a sensible wife.'

As Dan was the nearest to a bohemian she knew, at least being an artist, Joanna could only assume he was the friend her mother considered unsuitable.

Unfortunately—for her mother—she didn't agree with her. 'I doubt it, Mother,' she drawled. 'If you'll excuse me, I'll go and see what's keeping Joshua.' It had been at least half an hour since he had gone to the bathroom to shower.

She knocked lightly on the bedroom door, feeling a little stupid when he was her husband, but knowing she couldn't just walk in on him, not after all this time apart. When she received no answer to her second knock she softly opened the door, her eyes widening as she saw Joshua stretched out on the bed fast asleep, his only covering the chocolate brown sheet over his thighs.

She moved quietly into the room, closing the door behind her to stand beside the bed looking down at the man she loved. He looked younger in sleep, the lines of strain erased from his face, his hair still damp from his shower, his bare chest deeply bronzed, the hair there soft and silky.

Joanna drank her fill of him, loving every lithe muscular inch of him. She wouldn't give him up! Maybe tonight had been a bit of a disaster, but she wasn't going to meekly hand him over to Angela Hailey. The other woman had had him for the last year, and now *she* was taking over. She knew she hadn't imagined his physical response to her when he had held her in his arms earlier, and that was something to cling on to.

She touched his cheek with gentle fingertips, quickly removing her hand as he stirred in his sleep. But he only turned on to his side, taking the sheet with him, his long muscular legs bared too now. Joanna moved softly about the bed pulling the covers over him. After all, her flat might be warm, but it was the beginning of February.

She was smiling to herself as she left the bedroom, confident that tonight at least, Joshua would be staying at her flat.

CHAPTER SEVEN

JOSHUA was sitting at the breakfast bar in the kitchen the next morning when Joanna entered the room, forcing a casual smile to her lips as she moved to pour herself some coffee from the pot he had made. She looked slender and attractive in close-fitting cords and a blue silk blouse, having found the combination of the casual and smart an attractive one.

Joshua was watching her as she turned round, and she gave him a bright smile. 'Like some more coffee?' she indicated his empty mug.

'Thanks.' He stood up, his denims clinging revealingly to his muscular thighs and legs, the black turtle-necked sweater emphasising the width of his shoulders. He moved past her to pour his coffee, black and sweet, the way he liked it. 'Will Mr Cameron be joining us?' he turned to drawl, leaning back against the pine kitchen unit.

Joanna stiffened, frowning deeply. 'Dan? But he——'

'I hope I haven't inhibited your relationship with him,' Joshua mused. 'I was so tired last night that I fell asleep without meaning to.'

'Dan doesn't stay here,' she snapped, angry with him for thinking she would sleep with another man when her husband was in the same flat. She had got up with such a light heart this morning at the thought of Joshua being here that she had almost floated through her shower and getting dressed, and now he had dared to throw out an accusation like this!

His brows were raised over light grey eyes. 'He doesn't?'

'No!'

Joshua shrugged. 'Can I get you anything to eat? I hope you don't mind, I helped myself to some eggs and bacon from the fridge.'

'Be my guest!' Joanna was still angry with him for his wrong assumption about Dan and herself. And how could he go from talking about her supposed lover to offering to cook her breakfast! Did he really not care for her? She was beginning to think so.

'I am,' he smiled comfortably. 'I like your flat, Joanna, it's—relaxing.'

She felt her tension ease a little. 'I find it so,' she nodded.

'I have to go out today, so would you mind if I left my things here?'

She frowned, wondering when they were going to get round to the talk they were supposed to be having, although she understood that after a year away from London Joshua must have a lot of things to do. 'Of course,' she agreed to his request. 'I—Would you like to stay to dinner too?'

He drank the last of his coffee, putting the mug down on the worktop. 'That would be nice, thank you, Joanna.' He touched her cheek gently. 'I'll bring some wine back with me.'

She felt ridiculous standing in her kitchen with a silly smile on her face, her hand raised to the cheek Joshua had touched before he left, and yet she couldn't move for several minutes after he had gone. Finally it was the ringing of the telephone that broke her out of her reverie, and she moved to answer it.

'And how is the most beautiful child bride in the world this morning?' enquired a painfully cheerful voice.

'Dan!' she gasped in recognition of the only man mad

enough to talk to her this way. 'Joshua could have answered the telephone,' she complained impatiently.

'He could? I mean, *he could*?' Dan repeated speculatively.

She sighed at his wrong assumption. 'He slept in the spare room last night. From your good humour I gather that the second date worked out as you planned?' she snapped.

'Now, now, naughty, naughty,' he mocked. 'Don't take out your own frustration on poor Carmella and me!'

'Sorry.' She realised how bitchy she was being.

'Hah, so you are frustrated!' Dan pounced.

'No, I——'

'You mean Joshua spent the *whole* night in the spare room?' he continued as if she hadn't spoken.

'Yes,' she admitted miserably.

'Where is he now?'

'Out.'

'So it's safe to come round as usual?'

'It was safe for you to have spent the night here—in my room, if you'd wanted to.'

'It would have been a little crowded—Oh, I see, *me* and *you* in your bed,' he realised.

'You're so quick, Dan,' she derided.

'We are in a snappy mood today, aren't we?' he taunted. 'I'll be round in about an hour.'

'Won't Carmella mind?' she mocked.

He gave an exaggerated yawn. 'She had to leave early for a photographic session. It's a terrible life for us working people.'

'I know,' Joanna returned dryly. 'I'll expect you in an hour.'

'Joanna——!' Dan stopped her before she could ring off. 'Joshua isn't going to walk in and jump to conclusions, is he?'

'After what I just told you? He'll probably shake your hand and thank you for taking me off his hands,' she said bitterly.

Was it true? she wondered as she waited for Dan to arrive. Joshua hadn't seemed overly concerned at the idea of Dan having spent the night in her bed. If he cared that little about the thought of her with another man she could just be wasting her time even considering putting up a fight for him. Wasting her time or not, she was going to do it! Joshua was hers, and he was going to stay that way.

'Here's the next chapter for you to be working on.' She handed several typewritten sheets of paper to Dan when he arrived, pulling on her coat and hat, wrapping a scarf about her neck to keep out the cold February morning.

Dan frowned as he watched her. 'Where are you going?'

'Out,' she smiled at him.

'Very clever,' he derided. 'But I thought we were working this morning?'

'*You* are.' She picked up her bag, eyeing him mockingly as he gave an involuntary yawn. 'I'll lend you a couple of matchsticks too if you like.'

'Funny too,' he muttered. 'I'll be fine once I've had a couple of cups of your coffee. I trust you left some made in the kitchen?'

'Joshua did,' she nodded. 'And he makes it even stronger than I do.'

'Great,' he said with real enthusiasm. 'Jo, about last night——'

'It's private, Dan,' she told him lightly.

'Like that, hmm?' he accepted without rancour.

'Yes,' she said heavily. 'I wish it wasn't, I wish I could tell you that we've sorted out our differences and that we're back together. But we haven't and we aren't.'

'You still haven't told me where you're going this morning?' he frowned.

'Shopping.'

'Shopping? But James is waiting for this book——'

'I know,' she mocked. 'And I haven't forgotten the deadline, but you're a couple of chapters behind me anyway.'

'And I would get on a damn sight quicker if you stayed here and advised me,' he groaned.

'I'm not going on some frivolous spending spree, Dan,' she said impatiently. 'I'm going out to buy some food.'

'But you've already shopped for food this week——'

'Dan,' she interrupted softly, 'if I didn't know better I'd say you were acting like a complaining husband—— '

'And as Joanna still has a husband that could be a little difficult,' Joshua drawled as he walked in, Joanna having left the door open as she intended leaving immediately. He looked at their stricken faces in silent query. 'I forgot something from my suitcase,' he explained slowly as they both seemed to be struck dumb. 'I'll just get the papers and be on my way.' He turned towards the bedroom, his thigh-length sheepskin coat emphasising his height and breadth.

'No!' Joanna was galvanised into speech, a rose-tinted blush colouring her cheeks as Joshua turned back to her with raised brows. 'I—The two of you haven't been introduced properly.'

Mockery gleamed in the stormy grey eyes, Joshua looking very dark and attractive. 'I don't think that's necessary, Joanna, we each know who the other is.'

'Yes.' She chewed on her bottom lip. 'Er—Dan just came over to do some work.'

'Yes,' Joshua replied uninterestedly.

She gave a light, forced laugh. 'I'm afraid I had to drag him away from his girl-friend to get him here.'

A probing glance was turned on Dan, the grey eyes narrowing as Dan grinned at him goodnaturedly. 'I see,' he nodded. 'I won't keep you, then.' This time he went into the bedroom and closed the door.

Joanna swallowed hard, her breath leaving her in a sigh. 'Do you think he believed me?' she asked Dan anxiously.

He shrugged. 'You sounded a bit defensive to me, love——'

'Thanks!' she muttered badtemperedly. 'You realise he thinks you're my lover?'

'Mm, I'm flattered.'

'Dan——'

'Stop making such a fuss, Jo. He's been away with his girl-friend for the last year, remember,' he said pointedly.

All her anger left her. She had forgotten Angela Hailey for a few minutes. Joshua was probably spending the day with her.

'Hey, I'm sorry, sweet!' Dan exclaimed at her stricken look. 'But if you want him back, really want him back, you're going to have to fight for him in every feminine way possible. You know what I mean?' He spoke into her hair, so he couldn't see the bright colour in her cheeks.

'I know,' she mumbled.

'Don't tell me you don't want to, Jo.' He stroked her hair soothingly. 'I know physical desire when I see it.'

'Excuse me,' rasped the familiar voice of her husband. 'I didn't mean to interrupt your conversation, but—— Maybe I'd better give dinner a miss tonight, Joanna?' He looked at her with icy grey eyes.

She moved out of Dan's arms, her heart contracting painfully. 'You have another—appointment?' she asked huskily.

'No,' his gaze moved slowly to Dan, 'but I thought perhaps you had.'

She knew her laugh sounded hollow and false, but she couldn't find any genuine humour in the situation. 'Dan lives on baked beans and yoghurt. Decent food might throw his whole digestive system into a frenzy!'

Joshua's mouth twisted. 'So you won't be joining us, Mr Cameron?' he drawled.

'No,' Dan answered lightly. 'Will you be bringing Miss Hailey with you?'

Grey eyes turned metallic and then froze like silver ice. 'No,' Joshua bit out. 'Unless she was included in the invitation?' His gaze probed Joanna's pale face.

How could Dan do this to her, how *could* he mention Angela! 'No,' she said curtly, 'she wasn't.'

He nodded dismissively. 'I'll see you this evening, then. Cameron,' he added curtly to Dan before leaving.

'You big oaf!' Joanna turned on her red-haired tormentor as soon as they were alone. 'You idiot!' she hissed, punching him on the arm in her fury.

'Ouch!' He looked as if she had mortally wounded him. 'I was only trying to be helpful. How would you have felt if he'd turned up tonight at your cosy little dinner for two with his girl-friend in tow?'

She paled at the thought. 'Joshua may be hard, even a little cruel at times, but I can't believe he would ever do that to me.'

'He went off with her for a year, didn't he?'

She swallowed hard. 'That wasn't all his fault. I— He's a man——'

'I can see that!' he derided.

'And I wouldn't let him near me after Lindy died!

Surely you must realise how difficult that must have been for him.'

Dan's eyes widened. 'You're actually excusing what he did?' he said disbelievingly.

'I'm explaining it,' she corrected impatiently. 'We'd been married for three years before Lindy died, and our relationship was—well, it was——'

'Hot in bed,' he put in.

'Yes!' she glared at him. 'It was "hot in bed"! A man can't just switch off after three years like that.'

'Neither can a woman, not indefinitely.'

'I did.'

Dan shook his head. 'For that first year, maybe, but not after that. It wasn't lack of sexual interest that stopped you seeing other men this last year, it was lack of the right man.'

She blushed at his perception, at the lesson she had learnt on that last night with Joshua. If only he hadn't gone the next morning when she woke up, if only they could have talked——

'Live in the present, Jo,' Dan correctly read her soul-searching. 'Accept Joshua's affair for what it was, and then get your warpaint on.'

She smiled. 'I intend doing just that. You'll find the makings of a sandwich in the fridge if I'm not back by then—if you know how to make a sandwich, that is,' she derided.

'No baked beans?' he asked hopefully.

'I was only joking about that, Dan,' she laughed.

'I'm not,' he said dryly. 'A sandwich takes too much time to make and eat. Besides, I'm invited out to dinner tonight myself.'

'Carmella can cook too?' she teased.

He laughed his enjoyment. 'So she says. I'll let you know tomorrow. Or would you rather I gave tomorrow a miss?'

Joanna blushed at the devilment in his eyes. 'Call first, hmm?' She evaded his glance.

'I'll do that,' he said dryly. 'Now go and buy this gastronomic delight.'

'Roast chicken,' she corrected. 'It's Joshua's favourite.'

'Mine too,' he grinned.

'Tell that to Carmella!'

'Oh, I will,' he said with a wicked glint in his eye.

Joanna called in to see her parents at lunchtime after doing her shopping, and found both her mother and father in the lounge, but she refused their invitation to lunch.

'Is Joshua still at your flat?' her mother probed. 'Or have you both gone back to the house? We had so little opportunity to see him last night,' she added when Joanna confirmed that he was still at her flat.

'He was tired, Mother.'

'But you—spoke, later?'

'We talked this morning,' she said stiffly. 'Although not about anything important.'

'He looks well, anyway,' her father put in jovially.

'Well, of course he does, Gerald,' her mother snapped. 'He's just spent a year in the American sunshine. It's our little girl who has suffered this last year.'

Joanna grimaced at the sugary insincerity of her mother's words. Somewhere during the last year her mother had come round to the idea that Joanna was a deserted wife, that Joshua had no right leaving her the way he had. As with anything else her mother said nowadays, Joanna ignored it.

'Why don't the two of you come over to dinner?' her mother invited now. 'Then we can all have a talk together.'

'Cora——'

'We had intended to dine alone tonight,' Joanna frowned. 'I've just been out for the food.'

'Then I'm sure you bought enough for four. Your father and I will come over to you for dinner this evening.'

'But——'

'Cora, they want to be alone,' Joanna's father pointed out exasperatedly.

'Don't be silly, Gerald. You heard Joanna, they're still estranged.'

'Well, our presence isn't going to help matters,' he sighed.

'Joshua is our son-in-law,' her mother claimed in a hurt voice.

'And Joanna's husband,' her father defended. 'They need to be alone, to talk. We would only be in the way.'

'Well, really!' Her mother somehow managed to infuse hurt into her indignant exclamation, blinking back imaginary tears at the same time.

The selfish desire to be alone with Joshua warred with the possibility of alienating her mother for a few days or weeks. There was no doubt which one won. 'I really am sorry, Mother,' she stood up to leave, 'but I do want to be alone with Joshua tonight. Perhaps later in the week?' She caught her father's eye as he winked at her, seeing admiration for her in his expression.

'Perhaps,' her mother agreed haughtily. 'Well, we mustn't keep you, must we? I'm sure you want to get home.'

She held back her smile as her father winked at her once again. 'Yes, I do, actually,' she added fuel to the flame. 'I want to prepare the chicken.'

'Then don't let us keep you!'

Her father was the one to walk out to the car with

her, laughing softly as he did so. 'I love your mother, Joanna,' he chuckled, 'but sometimes she can be very insensitive. Have a nice dinner, darling,' he kissed her warmly on the cheek. 'And for goodness' sake don't forget to invite us to dinner when you and Joshua are feeling sociable again,' he warned.

'I won't,' she promised.

Her mother wasn't just insensitive, she was totally thoughtless. She was so curious to question Joshua herself that she cared nothing for the fact that Joanna and Joshua had been separated for a year, that they would have private things of their own to discuss.

She had never shared a moment of fun like that with her father before; it had given her a warm feeling to know that for once he understood her feelings and not her mother's.

She staggered into her flat with her bags of shopping to find Dan still at work on her long dining-room table, sketches scattered both there and on the floor.

He hadn't looked up when she came back from the kitchen after unpacking her shopping, bent over his latest sketch, a neat pile of them at his side ready to submit with her book for approval before he began work on the illustrations proper.

'If you're going to make a mess I wish you'd do it in your own flat.' She began to pick up the paper from the floor. She collected the mugs up from the table once she had disposed of the paper. 'Couldn't you at least have used the same one?' she groaned as she cleared away half a dozen dirty mugs.

'They aren't all mine,' he mumbled uninterestedly, concentrating on his latest sketch.

'They aren't?' Joanna frowned, halting on her way to the kitchen.

'No. Joshua came back and——'

'*Joshua* did?' The mugs rattled in her hands as she almost dropped them in her surprise. 'And you actually sat and drank coffee together?'

Dan looked up with a grin, giving her his full attention now. 'Well, it beats pistols any day.'

Joanna sat down shakily in one of the armchairs. 'Wh-what did you talk about?'

'The weather to start with. Then we got on to football, America——'

'Dan!'

'But we did,' he insisted.

'Football?' she derided. 'Joshua has never been interested in football.'

'Well, we definitely talked about it,' Dan shrugged. 'And he seemed to know what he was talking about too. He's quite a nice man once you get past that air of aloofness.'

'I wouldn't know,' she said stiffly. 'I never really got past it.'

'You must have done!'

'Not really,' she shook her head. 'Oh, at times I suppose I did, but I've always been a little—no, a *lot*, in awe of him.'

'Of your own husband?' Dan looked incredulous.

'You don't know all the circumstances, Dan.' She had never got around to telling Dan the reason Joshua had married her.

'I'd love to hear them some time.' He gave her an avid look.

'Well, you aren't going to.' She stood up determinedly. 'Now get your things together and go home; I have to get my dinner on.'

'So nice to be wanted!'

'Er—Why did Joshua come back this time?' Joanna lingered on in the room.

'Would you believe, he forgot something else?' Dan taunted mockingly.

Joanna frowned; a forgetful memory had never been something Joshua had suffered from in the past. But then he had changed a lot this last year; he seemed more relaxed, less the aloof stranger he had become before he left for the States. If he had spoken to Dan about football he had certainly changed; the sport had never interested him in the past.

'I'm going now.' Dan came into the kitchen to see her a few minutes later. 'Have a good evening.' He kissed her lightly on the cheek.

'You too,' she smiled.

'Oh, I will,' he grinned. 'By the way, I gave Joshua that spare key to the flat you leave on the hook over there,' he added as an afterthought.

Joanna frowned, glancing at the empty hook next to the cooker. 'Did he ask for it?'

'No. But he can hardly keep knocking for entrance to his own wife's home, now can he?' Dan derided.

'No, I—I suppose not,' she answered in a preoccupied voice. 'Did he say what time he would be back?'

'Nope. And I didn't ask him,' Dan grinned. 'None of my business, is it? But I did emphasise the fact that I have a very heated relationship going with Carmella.'

She evaded his gaze, unwilling to show how much his next answer mattered to her. 'What was his reaction?'

'He didn't have one,' Dan told her cheerfully. 'See you tomorrow.' He was whistling tunelessly as he left.

He didn't have one! Could Joshua really be so uninterested in what she had been doing, who she had been seeing for the last year?

She was in her bedroom changing for dinner when she heard his key in the door, and her breath caught in her throat just at the thought of seeing him again. She had chosen to wear a royal blue silky shirtwaister dress, its tie emphasising the narrowness of her waist and slender hips. Her hair was soft and newly washed, her make-up light, the plum-coloured lipgloss clearly outlining the provocative pout of her lips.

'I'm back, Joanna.' He knocked lightly on her bedroom door, just the sound of his voice increasing her heart-rate.

She opened the bedroom door to him; his expression was enigmatic as he looked down at her. 'Just in time for dinner,' she told him brightly, determined to act natural tonight. 'It should be ready in about half an hour.'

He nodded, the sheepskin jacket already discarded, his black clothing suiting his rugged good looks. 'I'll just shower and change, then.'

A mental picture of the dinners they used to share, with Joshua all stiff and formal in a dinner suit and herself coldly sophisticated, flashed into her mind. 'Joshua!' she blushed as he turned back from entering the spare bedroom. 'I—Wear something casual, hmm?' She watched him anxiously as she waited for his reaction.

His brow cleared of the frown that had appeared when she called his name, an amused smile curved his lips. 'I don't have anything else with me,' he explained. 'I left all my dinner suits at the house when I left.'

'Oh, good. I mean——'

'You mean "oh, good",' he drawled as she blushed again. 'You're looking very beautiful tonight, Joanna,' he told her softly. 'That shade of blue suits you.'

Joanna was still filled with the happy glow his compliment had caused when he joined her in the kitchen twenty minutes later, his only concession to formality being that his shirt was buttoned almost up to his throat. Almost, but not quite; a temptingly soft tendril of wiry hair was still visible at the vee-neckline. Joanna drank in his appearance like a thirsty man drinks water after coming out of a desert, loving the way the navy blue cords clung to his long legs and thighs, the lighter blue shirt making his eyes appear almost the same colour.

He grimaced as she continued to stare at him, misunderstanding her fixed gaze. 'I'm afraid I've become very casual during my year in America. Even a business suit can occasionally look overdressed over there.'

'Oh no, you look—you look very nice,' she amended the 'wonderful' she had been going to use to describe his appearance. 'Please go through to the lounge and pour yourself a drink.'

'No, thanks.' He lounged against the kitchen unit closest to her as she worked at the cooker. 'Dinner smells good.'

'Thank you.' Once again she blushed at his compliment, feeling slightly unnerved by his closeness. 'Are you sure you wouldn't like a drink?' She could smell his aftershave, loved the way his hair curled damply about his ears and nape, had difficulty resisting the impulse to touch that hair, to run her fingers through it as she pressed her mouth against his.

His dark brows rose at her flustered attitude. 'Am I in your way?' he mused.

'Er—no. No, of course not,' she insisted vehemently. 'I just thought——'

'I am in your way,' he drawled with a twist of his mouth, pushing away from the kitchen unit with a ripple of muscle. 'I'll go and sit in the lounge.'

Joanna would have liked to ask him to stay, would have enjoyed just having him close to her. And yet she knew she would ruin their dinner if Joshua stayed here watching over her in the crucial stages of the meal.

He was sprawled in an armchair, his eyes closed, one ankle crossed over the other as she carried their laden plates through to the dining-room. His eyes flickered open as he heard her approach, drawing in his stretched legs so that she could get by.

'I left the wine in the fridge to cool.' He stood up. 'I'll go and get it.'

She had forgotten about the wine he had promised to bring, and she went to get out the glasses while he took the cork out of the wine and brought the bottle through. She sipped at the chilled white wine with a shaking hand. It was ridiculous, she felt as if she were out on her first date with Joshua instead of having been married to him for six years. She wondered if he felt the same way; he certainly didn't look in the least nervous or disconcerted as he sat across from her to eat his meal.

'You never told me you could cook like this,' he said after several silent minutes eating.

The high colour wouldn't seem to fade from her cheeks. 'I learnt at school.'

'It's good to have a home-cooked meal after living in hotels for a year,' he added appreciatively, filling up her wine glass when it was only half empty, his hand strong and capable, the gold watch she had bought him for Christmas one year glinting amongst the dark hair on his wrist.

'You lived the whole year in hotels?' She couldn't hide her surprise. 'I somehow thought you and Angela——' She broke off, biting her lower lip, in anger, with herself for mentioning the other woman. The evening had been going so well, why did she have to spoil it by mentioning his mistress!

'Yes?' Joshua looked unperturbed by her slip.

She glanced away. 'I thought you might have rented a house or an apartment some of the time,' she finished awkwardly.

'There wasn't time,' he shrugged, sitting back to sip his wine. 'I don't think you would have liked the constant moving about, Joanna.'

She hadn't been given the chance to either like or dislike anything! She had known on that last morning when she woke up after a night in his arms that she would follow him anywhere. But he hadn't wanted her, had gone off with his mistress as if nothing had changed.

'Probably not,' she agreed stiffly, taking a couple of large swallows of her wine, feeling nothing as the cold alcohol hit her stomach. 'Did you go to the house at all today?' she changed the subject.

'Only to get the car. When I got to the house I found I'd left my keys here, and Mrs Barnaby seems to have misplaced the spare set.'

'Oh no, I have them,' she assured him. 'You left them on my dressing-table that last nigh—Well, you left them in my room,' she mumbled. 'I put them in my handbag, they're still there.'

Again his expression remained bland. 'I talked to Dan when I got back,' he told her coolly.

Not Cameron, or Mr Cameron, but *Dan*! Perhaps the two men really had discussed football and the weather!

'He gave me your spare key,' Joshua murmured. 'I hope you don't mind.'

'Not at all.' She put her glass down, only to have Joshua instantly fill it up again. At this rate she was going to be drunk at the end of dinner. 'I would have given it to you myself if I'd thought of it.'

'Thanks,' he nodded. 'Dan tells me the fourth book is near to completion?'

'Another couple of days and we should be finished,' she nodded.

'Got any more lined up?'

'A couple,' she acknowledged. 'Mother thinks it's scandalous that I actually get paid for writing about a dog!'

'Not just any dog,' Joshua said softly. 'Your dog. You loved him very much, didn't you? It came over in your books,' he explained.

'Yes, I loved him very much,' Joanna admitted huskily. 'Would you like some dessert?' He had eaten all the roast she had given him, although some food still remained on her own plate; she was too nervous to have much of an appetite.

'Thanks.' He stood up to help her clear the table. 'Why didn't you ever get another dog?'

She laughed lightly. 'Billy was a mistake as far as my mother was concerned, another dog would have been a disaster!'

'I suppose so,' he nodded. 'Billy sounds as if he was a bit of a handful,' he smiled.

Her heart did a somersault at the sight of that devastating smile, she swallowed heavily. 'He was,' she confirmed throatily. 'Most boxers are. Another dog could never have taken his place anyway,' she shrugged dismissal, and went through to the kitchen to get the lemon meringue pie she had made for dessert, another of Joshua's favourites.

'I'll be putting on weight.' He sat back replete after refusing a third piece of pie.

'You're probably too thin at the moment.' She cleared away the debris from their meal, putting all the crockery into the dishwasher.

'So are you.' He had followed her, looking at her critically as she moved about the kitchen. 'How much weight have you lost?' he frowned.

Once again she couldn't meet his gaze. 'About ten pounds. But it's fashionable.'

'I prefer you a little—meatier,' he shrugged.

Joanna instantly decided to put the weight back on no matter what she had to eat to do it! She wanted to be just as Joshua liked her, wanted to *please* him.

They listened to records in favour of television once they returned to the lounge, sitting side by side on the sofa, Joshua's arm resting lightly along the back behind Joanna. He didn't actually touch her, and yet she couldn't have been more aware of him if he had been.

The silence between them stretched out as one record after another was played on her stereo system, and finally Joanna could stand it no longer. He would probably be leaving soon, and so far he had made no mention of seeing her again after tonight.

'Do you——'

'Have you——' They both began talking at the same time. 'You first,' Joshua invited ruefully.

She looked up at him with luminous blue eyes. 'It wasn't really important.'

He seemed fascinated by her parted lips. 'Neither was what I was going to say,' he said huskily.

'Oh.'

'Joanna!' The arm behind her moved as his hand clasped about her nape, pulling her slowly towards him. 'Say no if you want to.' His mouth was only inches away from hers, his eyes stormy, his voice a low groan.

'Yes,' she breathed softly.

With a muffled moan his mouth claimed hers, probing gently, searchingly, his lips moving slowly with hers in a kiss that devoured and ignited deeper passion, although he didn't deepen it, made no effort to do more than kiss her, her own pleading groans in her throat doing nothing to incite the heady possession she craved.

She was flushed and breathing heavily by the time he put her away from him, his eyes enigmatic, his expression unrevealing. She quivered as he smoothed the hair back from her face, raining light kisses across her cheek and down to her ear, biting gently on the lobe before searching the hollows of her throat with a probing tongue, making her tremble with wanting.

And still he controlled both their responses, his mouth returning to hers to kiss her deeply, hungrily, the tip of his tongue running lightly along her lips, resisting all her efforts to have him probe her mouth further, to give her satisfaction in that way, to reveal that his desire for her equalled her own for him.

She leant weakly against him as he moved back from her, his hands on her shoulders sitting her back on her side of the sofa, only the stormy colour of his eyes telling of his own response.

He stood up to look down at her. 'Do you still take sugar in your coffee?' he asked huskily.

'Coffee?' she blinked, too dazed by his kisses to think straight at the moment.

'Yes. Do you still take sugar?' His voice was hard.

'Yes. But——' before she could say any more he had gone into the kitchen.

Her hands clenched into fists of agony, of physical pain, of her instant arousal and Joshua's rejection of her obvious reaction. What was he trying to do to her? Had he been playing with her, was it an experiment on his part to see if he was still attracted to her? If it had been she had failed him, she had failed them both.

'Here you are.' He handed her one of the mugs of coffee he was carrying, frowning as he saw how pale her face was. 'Are you okay?' He sat down beside her once again.

'Fine.' She forced a smile to her lips. 'Maybe a little tired.'

He nodded. 'I'll leave as soon as I've drunk my coffee.'

Joanna swallowed hard as he confirmed her suspicion that he intended leaving. She had somehow hoped—But why should he want to stay on here, especially after tonight's fiasco?

They drank their coffee in silence, a silence Joanna felt too miserable to break, and one Joshua didn't seem to want to break. He was probably just trying to finish his coffee and leave! Oh God, what a mess!

He took their empty mugs back into the kitchen. 'I'll just go and get my things.'

He was walking out on her for a second time and there wasn't a thing she could do to stop it! She couldn't even persuade him to make love to her this time.

But none of her dejection showed when Joshua came back with his single suitcase, pulling on his sheepskin jacket. She walked with him to the door, a bright smile fixed to her lips.

One of his hands moved up to cup her cheek, his thumbtip moving gently over her lips. 'Have dinner with me tomorrow night?' he encouraged throatily.

Her eyes widened as she almost gaped at him. 'D-dinner?'

'Yes,' he smiled. 'It's the least I can do after you fed me this evening. We'll go out somewhere, hmm?'

Why couldn't she stop smiling like an idiot— Joshua was going to think she was cracking up! 'Dinner would be lovely, thank you,' she accepted casually.

'I'll see you about eight o'clock.' With one last fleeting caress of her lips with his he was gone.

It was only later, as she lay in bed alone, that she realised Joshua hadn't returned the key to her flat. The thought warmed her.

CHAPTER EIGHT

IT was a little strange to think of going out on a date with your own husband. Joanna felt a little as she had on her first ever date when she was sixteen, only this time it wasn't with freckle-faced John Larner, it was with Joshua, and even to think of the two men in the same breath was like comparing a kitten and a roaring lion. She felt as nervous as a kitten herself, discarding everything in her wardrobe as unsuitable, and deciding she would have to buy something new to wear.

She was critical of everything she tried on in the salon; nothing was just right, nothing perfect enough for an evening with Joshua. Then she saw it, a beautiful red dress, with a fitted tight bodice, very narrow ribbon straps, the tight waist flowing in soft folds to the ragged gypsy-style hemline just below her knees. It was exactly what she was looking for, totally feminine, the tightness of the bodice pushing her breasts up so that their gentle curve was revealed temptingly to anyone who cared to look or come close enough. She hoped she could interest Joshua enough for that, intended using all her feminine wiles to fight for him as Dan had advised her to.

Dan was sitting on her doorstep when she arrived home. Not literally of course, she didn't have a doorstep, but he was doing a good job of propping up the wall.

'Where have you been?' he scowled. 'I called over an hour ago, and when there was no answer I decided to come over.'

147

'What's your panic?' She tucked her dress-box under one arm so that she could get her key out of her bag, handing it to Dan as she balanced her shoe-box in the other hand, the sandals a perfect match in colour for the dress.

'James wants to see us.' He threw himself into one of the armchairs once they were inside, glancing at his wrist-watch. 'Ten minutes ago,' he grimaced.

Joanna frowned, putting her parcels down. 'What's his panic?'

'I haven't liked to mention it, but you do realise what tomorrow is, don't you?' He gave her a searching look.

'Tomorrow? Why, it's—Oh,' she grimaced. 'He's waiting for the book, right?'

'Expecting it is more the impression I got,' Dan told her ruefully. 'And we still have the last few pages to do.'

'Damn!' She chewed on her bottom lip. 'It's all up here,' she tapped her head. 'I just have to get it down on paper.'

Joshua sighed. 'You know James, he isn't the most patient or forgiving of men. We promised him the complete book by tomorrow, and that's when he'll want it.'

She did know how tough James Colnbrook could be, and had wondered since she had got to know him better how she had got away with her treatment of him the first time they met. She had finally put it down to the fact that he had been so dumbfounded by the totally controlled bitch she had been then that he had been rendered speechless. Whatever the reason for his forbearance then it didn't apply now; a deadline on a book was sacrosanct to James, with no excuses accepted.

'Maybe if we worked all night——'

'I have a date tonight!' she told him desperately.

'And you think I don't?' Dan bit out angrily. 'Carmella isn't the sort of woman you call up and put off for a date; she's likely to go out and find herself someone else—and preferably not an illustrator of children's books who's broke most of the time.'

Joanna accepted the rebuke in the gentle way it was given. She had been selfish the last couple of weeks, her attention all on Joshua's possible return and not on the fact that the deadline for the fourth book was nearing. She might have money of her own, but Dan was a working man, and she owed him the professional respect of doing her side of the work on time. She had held him up with her preoccupation with Joshua, and now she would have to make up for it.

'I'll call Joshua and explain to him that I have to work,' she told Dan.

'Joshua?' he frowned. 'You were going out on a date with your husband?'

'Yes.'

'He isn't staying here?'

'He went back to the house,' she avoided Dan's gaze. 'I'll just put these things away and then I'll call him.'

'Jo——'

'It's all right, Dan,' she smiled at him. 'If you can make the sacrifice so can I. Call Carmella now and explain if you like.'

He nodded, already dialling. 'But she isn't going to like it,' he sighed.

Joanna had no idea what Joshua's reaction was going to be. Her own was one of dread. Suppose he didn't ask to see her again when she had to put him off for tonight? That possibility didn't bear thinking about.

As soon as she knew Dan was off the telephone in the lounge she called the house from her bedroom extension, wanting privacy for her conversation with

Joshua. She was frowning heavily when she came back from the bedroom.

'Carmella was fine about it,' Dan grinned, his good spirits obviously restored.

'Good,' she replied in a preoccupied voice.

'I hope you don't mind, but she was so disappointed that our date was off for tonight that I invited her here instead.'

'Here?' That broke Joanna out of her reverie. 'You invited her here, Dan?'

'Yes. You see——'

'But she's going to be bored out of her mind sitting here all evening while we work,' she groaned. 'You know you don't even hear people once you get started!'

'I hear Carmella,' he told her quietly, with sincerity. 'Jo, I think she's the one.'

'I don't—You do?' Her voice softened interestedly.

He grinned at her surprise. 'I do. She's beautiful, intelligent, and good in——'

'Yes, Dan,' she interrupted dryly. 'I think we can all guess what she's good at. What time is she arriving?'

'In time for the pizza I'll order to be delivered for seven-thirty.'

Joanna grimaced. A pizza hadn't been what she had in mind for her dinner, but then neither was spending the evening with Dan and his girl-friend. 'Okay,' she sighed, 'let's get to work. Even a rough draft would keep James happy for now.'

'We hope. He wasn't too happy when I spoke to him just now and told him we wouldn't be in with the book this afternoon.' Dan pulled a face.

'You called him too?' Joanna gasped.

'Yes,' he nodded. 'Well, someone had to; we should have been there ages ago. How did your call to Joshua go?'

She swallowed hard, suddenly preoccupied with her notes. 'It didn't,' she mumbled.

But Dan heard her anyway. 'Didn't what?' he prompted.

'Didn't go,' she answered briskly. 'Joshua wasn't at the house.'

'But you left a message for him?'

'I—I couldn't,' she choked, tears in her eyes as she finally met Dan's gaze. 'He isn't at the house, he hasn't been back there since yesterday afternoon!'

She had hardly been about to believe it when Mrs Barnaby told her that Joshua wasn't staying at the house, that she hadn't seen him since he had collected the Rolls yesterday. It didn't need two guesses where he had been all night, and the thought of him going from her to Angela nearly killed her.

'Now don't jump to conclusions——'

'Conclusions?' she echoed Dan tautly. 'He left here late last night, and I—I assumed he'd gone home. Where else could he have gone except to Angela?'

'Any number of places,' Dan shrugged.

'Name one!'

'Well, a club——'

'He doesn't have one!'

'A friend's—I said a friend, Jo,' he reproved. 'Not a mistress.'

'He went to her,' she choked. 'I know he did!'

'I can see there's no talking you out of it,' Dan sighed at her vehemence. 'But if you didn't get to talk to him that means he's still going to arrive here tonight expecting to take you out.'

'Yes . . .' she realised, blinking back the tears.

'I'd better make sure I order enough pizza for four,' he said cheerfully. 'What a happy little group we're going to be,' he added derisively.

There was no question of wearing the red dress that evening, designer jeans and a red silk blouse were the nearest she came to looking elegant. Carmella was similarly attired when she arrived shortly after seven.

Joanna hadn't had much opportunity to talk to the other woman at her party the other evening, and far from being one of Dan's usual women with no brains and a fantastic body Carmella turned out to be vivacious and amusing too.

'I hope you don't mind Dan inviting me here?' she asked once the initial greetings were over.

'Not at all,' Joanna smiled. 'My husband should be here soon too.' She just hoped he would stay when he arrived.

'Your husband . . .? Oh yes,' Carmella nodded. 'The handsome devil that arrived in the middle of the party the other night. Down, boy!' she teased Dan as he gave a jealous growl at her from his position at the dining-room table. 'I was only window-shopping, not buying.'

Joanna laughed at Dan's dumbfounded expression, enjoying seeing him being the one who was tormented for a change.

'Joshua isn't for sale,' Dan drawled. 'He's very much a married man.'

If only that were true! Joanna could feel her tension rising as the minutes ticked by to eight o'clock, horrified at the thought of Joshua being with Angela last night, and yet terrified at the thought of not seeing him again.

When the doorbell rang at five to eight she knew it had to be him, and she felt rooted to the spot. What if he became angry at the other couple being here and walked off? What if he——

'Aren't you going to answer that?' Dan looked up from his work with a frown.

'I—Of course.' She wiped her suddenly damp hands down her denim-clad thighs. 'Yes, of course,' she said more firmly, and went out into the hallway as the doorbell rang again.

Joshua's eyes widened as he took in her casual appearance, his brows raised questioningly as her bottom lip began to tremble. He looked so achingly attractive in a navy blue suit, although the dark hair still hadn't been cut to his usual shorter style.

'I had booked a table at Frederico's,' he murmured slowly. 'But if you'd rather eat somewhere less formal . . .?'

Her present clothing was completely unsuitable to go to the famous London restaurant, and her mouth quivered even more. 'I can't go, Joshua!' she burst out emotionally. 'Tomorrow is the deadline for my book and Dan and I have to work all night to get it finished!' She looked up at him miserably.

His eyes narrowed as he thrust his hands into his trouser pockets, pulling the material tautly across his powerful thighs. 'You and Dan,' he repeated softly. 'And you'll be—working, all night?'

She missed that deliberate pause in his speech in her own agitation, sure that he was just going to turn around and leave. 'Yes. I tried to call you, but Mrs Barnaby says you haven't been back to the house.' The statement was made in the form of a question.

'That's right.' His answer wasn't forthcoming. 'I'd better leave you and Dan to get on with your work, then,' he said coldly.

'Oh, but—We're all going to have pizza and coffee for dinner,' she rushed into speech, saying anything to stop him walking away. 'Why don't you join us?' She almost groaned her embarrassment as she heard herself inviting Joshua to share a pizza and coffee for his dinner; it was like inviting royalty to eat fish and chips out of a newspaper!

'All?' he frowned.

'Yes, Dan's girl-friend Carmella is here too,' she explained eagerly. At least he hadn't turned her invitation down cold! 'I'm sure she would appreciate your company while Dan and I work—if you wouldn't mind, that is,' she added awkwardly, making a complete mess of her invitation, making it sound as if she just wanted him to come in so that he could amuse Carmella. She didn't want that at all, would much rather have spent the evening alone with him, and if Carmella appreciated his company too much everyone was going to find that out.

He seemed to hesitate for long timeless seconds, then he nodded. 'Pizza and coffee sound fine,' he accepted lightly.

'Oh, good!' Relief flooded through her as she opened the door wider. 'Come in—Dan is just about to order the pizza.'

'With mushrooms, I hope,' Joshua drawled to Dan as he strolled into the lounge, removing his sheepskin jacket to reveal the jacket to his suit, removing that too and giving them both to Joanna as she put her hand out for them.

'Oodles of them,' Carmella smiled over at him warmly. 'I love them too.'

Joanna threw Joshua's coat and jacket across the bed with little regard for their welfare, hurrying back to the lounge before Carmella could flirt with him any more. The two of them were bent over her record collection, Carmella's denims tighter even then her own, her black top figure-hugging, leaving her shoulders and arms bare. Joshua had removed his tie and undone the top two buttons of his shirt, looking very relaxed and at ease. He had never looked that way with her.

'Let's get to work, Jo.'

She turned to find Dan looking at her pointedly, flushing at the mocking way he raised his eyebrows. With one last look at the dark head bent over the fiery red one she turned to join Dan.

Carmella's throaty laugh rang out several times during the next half hour as they waited for the food to be delivered, and each time it did Joanna looked over at the other couple. They were sitting one each end of the sofa, talking softly, both looking as if they were enjoying themselves as they chatted together and sipped the drinks they had poured.

'They're only talking, Jo,' Dan told her softly as she looked up for what must have been the sixth time in a matter of minutes.

She blushed as she realised he must have been watching her. 'I can't help it,' she muttered. 'He never sat and talked with me like that.'

'Maybe he didn't think you wanted him to,' Dan shrugged.

'That's ridiculous!'

'Is it?' Dan chided. 'I seem to remember you were rather a cool young woman when we met a year ago. Quite formidable!'

'I was what he made me!' Her eyes flashed.

'And he's what you made him! You know your problem, Jo, you're each afraid to communicate to the other——'

'Joshua isn't frightened of anything!'

He glanced over to where the other couple still chatted amiably together, seemingly unaware of the heated conversation taking place across the room from them. 'Everyone is afraid of something, Jo,' Dan turned back to her. 'Even Joshua. And you're terrified he's going to end your marriage.'

'Wouldn't you be?'

'Maybe,' he sighed. 'But believe me, Carmella is no threat to you as far as Joshua is concerned.'

Her mouth twisted. 'You have her so enthralled with you that she can't see anyone else, hmm?' she attempted to tease, realising she was behaving stupidly. Of course Joshua was being friendly with Carmella—the two of them could hardly have sat in silence all evening. But did Joshua have to look as if he were enjoying himself as much? a mental tormenter asked, his husky laugh as frequent as Carmella's.

'Of course,' Dan played along. 'It's my beautiful body that does it.'

'Does what, darling?' Unnoticed by either of them, Carmella had strolled over to join them, catching the tail-end of the conversation, her hand caressing on Dan's shoulder, an intimacy he obviously enjoyed, as he smiled up at her with a shared warmth.

Joanna glanced at Joshua, wishing she had the nerve to perform such an intimacy on him, blushing as she found him looking back at her with hooded eyes.

'Keeps women attracted to me,' Dan explained with a grin, drawing Joanna's attention back to him. 'I have this wonderful power over them with my body.'

'That's what you think!' Carmella laughed at him. 'It's the women who control the men, isn't it, Joanna?' she looked at Joanna for support.

'I—er—I——'

'Don't be modest, darling.' Joshua was at her side as she blushed painfully, his arm going about her shoulders. 'You know it's true.' He smiled down at her, a warm and loving smile to anyone looking on, although Joanna knew he was only helping her through an embarrassing moment. They both knew she had never been able to hold him in any way, least of all physically, and that even the previous evening he had been able to walk away from her when he must have known she would much rather he had stayed and made love to her.

Luckily the pizza arrived at that moment to save her any more embarrassment, and the subject was forgotten as they ate and drank their dinner. The conversation was light and teasing, and Joanna glimpsed a side of Joshua she had never seen before, a part of him that could be teased, the teasing being accepted in the light spirit that it was given.

She didn't resent the murmured conversation between Joshua and Carmella after they had eaten, knowing by Dan and Carmella's manner towards each other that they really were very attracted to each other, and that, for the moment at least, Carmella wasn't interested in any other man except Dan.

With that worry off her mind she was able to concentrate on her work, just content to have Joshua in the same room as her. Dan raised his brows at her sudden burst of inspiration, but made no comment as to the reason for it.

'Finished!' Dan finally sat back with a sigh just after twelve, running a tired hand around the back of his nape. 'You too?' He looked at Joanna.

'Yes.' Her sigh was just as weary. 'I just hope James appreciates our efforts.'

'I doubt it,' he grimaced, and stood up, flexing his aching shoulder muscles.

'Finished, darling?' Carmella looked over at them. She and Joshua had lapsed into a comfortably silence long ago, listening to the softly playing stereo.

'I hope so,' he smiled. 'I'm too tired to do any more.' He pulled on the jacket he had discarded when they began work. 'Feel like going to a party, Carmella?'

'Love to. But——'

'A private party,' he grinned. 'Just the two of us.'

'Lovely!' She stood up eagerly.

'You see,' Dan told the other two mockingly, 'it's the thought of the body that does it.'

'The thought of sleep is nearer the truth,' Carmella said dryly. 'I have been up since six this morning, you know.'

'So have I; you made me get your breakfast, remember?'

The other couple were still gently arguing as they left a few minutes later, the closeness of their relationship obvious. Joanna looked awkwardly at Joshua once they were alone, surprised that he had stayed this long; after all, it must be a strange way for him to spend his evening.

'I'm sorry——'

'I've enjoyed this evening, Joanna,' he firmly interrupted her apology. 'But I had no idea you had to work so hard.' He stood up as she walked over to join him, taking her hand to pull her gently down on the couch beside him, holding her close to his side. 'I don't remember you having to do so much on the first book. Or was it just that I was always out at work?' he added ruefully.

She was breathless from being this close to him, from the way his thumb seemed to be absently caressing the back of her hand. 'No—of course not,' she answered. 'I did a lot of it after—after you had gone. James was just being kind at the first interview I had with him, there was quite a lot of rewriting to to be done.'

'You and Dan seem to work well together.' He released her hand to put his arm about her shoulders, his hand beneath the hair at her nape.

'Yes. But——'

'I wasn't implying anything else,' he smiled gently. 'Dan went out of his way yesterday to tell me you're friends and work colleagues, nothing else, and that you never have been. So if not Dan, did you see other men this last year?' he probed softly.

'I—saw some, yes,' she looked down at her hands, talking slowly, 'but nothing serious.'

'No lovers?'

Hot colour flooded her cheeks. 'None!' she flashed.

'Look at me, Joanna.'

She could do nothing else at the sound of his throatily pleading voice, looking up to find herself drowning in the liquid warmth of his eyes. 'Joshua . . .' she had time to groan before his mouth came down on hers.

It was as if they had both been waiting for this moment all evening. Joanna fell back against the cushions of the sofa, Joshua following her tonight, his mouth still moving against hers, moist and soft, devouring.

She laced her fingers in the springy cleanliness of his thick dark hair, determined he wasn't going to leave her this time, holding him to her, kissing him with a hunger that he couldn't misinterpret.

He didn't seem to want to; his lips probing the warmth of her mouth, engaging in a battle with her that could have only one ending, one they both knew Joanna wasn't really fighting.

'You're beautiful, Joanna,' he murmured against her throat. 'More beautiful than I even remembered. Darling . . .!' He slipped her blouse off one shoulder, the buttons falling undone as his hand slipped down to her waist, finding no obstacle to his questing fingers as he cupped her naked breasts. 'That's new,' he murmured, his lips against her creamy flesh. 'Not that you ever needed a bra. You're perfect, Joanna. Perfect ...' his mouth closed over one taut nipple, the wild sensation this evoked making her feel weak with longing.

She wanted to touch him, *needed* to touch him in return, and her hands slipped beneath the silky shirt, the last of the buttons easily undone as she sought that closer contact with him. Their skins seemed to sear together as Joshua began to kiss her once again, deep hungry kisses that had them both trembling within minutes, the hair on Joshua's chest abrasive against her sensitive breasts.

He stopped her hands as she would have explored his thighs the way he was caressing hers through the denim of her jeans. 'No ...' he groaned.

'Yes!' she pleaded, evading his grasp, loving the way his body leapt with desire as she touched him, revelling in the mastery it gave her. 'It is the women who control, isn't it?' she said wonderingly as he shuddered beneath her hand.

'Have you only just discovered that?' Joshua moaned huskily.

No, she had always known it, even as a young siren of seventeen she had known how to arouse Joshua so deeply he just had to make love to her. As she wanted him to make love to her now!

But he was already pushing her away from him, rebuttoning his shirt as he stood up to tuck it back into the waistband of his trousers, his thighs still taut with desire.

'You—you aren't leaving?' Her eyes were the deep blue of a stormy sky.

'It's almost one o'clock,' he told her, shrugging into his jacket and coat.

Joanna swallowed convulsively, more confused and hurt than she had been the evening before. How was she failing him? What was she doing wrong?

'You should get to bed, Joanna,' he told her abruptly now. 'Didn't Dan mention something about an appointment with your publisher tomorrow?'

'That isn't until the afternoon,' she dismissed. 'After tonight I'll probably spend the morning in bed. Joshua——'

'I have to go,' he said briskly.

'I—You—Are you staying at a hotel?' She moistened her lips nervously as she realised she was just asking for a set-down. Joshua didn't have to tell her where he was staying. 'I thought you said you were tired of them——'

'I am,' he said patiently. 'And I'm not staying at one.' He seemed to hesitate. 'I'm staying with a friend,' he revealed with reluctance.

'Oh,' she breathed raggedly. 'Well, I mustn't keep you, then.'

'We missed our dinner tonight,' he said abruptly. 'Could you make it tomorrow instead?'

'Tomorrow? But—er—Won't your—friend mind?' she frowned.

'No,' he smiled. 'And although I enjoyed the pizza it wasn't really what I had in mind for us.'

Us. How good that sounded! And if Joshua chose to take her out rather than spend the time with his mistress that was his business. 'Dinner tomorrow would be lovely,' she accepted with undisguised pleasure.

'Then do up your blouse and walk me to the door,' he laughed softly at her embarrassed flush as she quickly rebuttoned her blouse. 'You would never make a femme fatale, my darling,' he teased indulgently.

If he hadn't tagged that endearment on the end of that statement Joanna could have been quite hurt. As it was she just glowed up at him, finishing buttoning her blouse with deft fingers as she walked with him to the door.

'Is eight o'clock okay again for tomorrow?' he prompted softly.

'Fine,' she nodded. 'And this time I promise Dan and Carmella won't be waiting too.'

He smiled. 'I quite enjoyed this evening. But I would rather be alone with you.'

She moved into his arms with natural grace, returning his kiss with a fervour that made him groan his own response against her lips, kissing her deeply, his body leaping in response.

'Stay,' she pleaded against his lips. 'Stay with me tonight, Joshua!'

'I can't.' He pulled away from her, holding her at arm's length. 'I'm expected, Joanna.'

There wasn't even regret in his voice, just calm reasoning. Once again he was going from her to Angela. And there seemed to be nothing she could do about it. He desired her, he couldn't deny his bodily response, but it wasn't enough, it still wasn't enough.

But she was seeing him again tomorrow. Maybe then he wouldn't leave her at the end of the evening, maybe then he wouldn't want to leave her again.

CHAPTER NINE

DUE to lack of sleep the night before, and the fact that
she had worked so intensely during the evening, Joanna
overslept the next day. Finally it was the ringing of the
doorbell that woke her, and she crawled out of bed to
stagger out of her room to answer the door.

'Dan, I—Joshua!' Her eyes widened at the fact that it
was her husband standing in front of her and not Dan
at all. She looked down selfconsciously at her night-
shirt, feeling very juvenile in its masculine styling. 'I—
er—I overslept,' she pushed back her hair. 'I—What do
you have there?' she frowned as the front of his coat
seemed to be emitting a strange sound, moving as she
watched him.

'A kitten.' He pulled the tiny black kitten from the
depths of his jacket, holding the tiny fluffy creature as it
looked at Joanna with bright button-black eyes. 'Do
you mind if I—we come in?' He raised dark brows.

'Of course.' She opened the door for him to enter,
following slowly, still not properly awake. The reason
for Joshua having a kitten was beyond her at the
moment. 'Where did you get it, Joshua?' she frowned.

'Don't you like him?' His expression was softened as
he placed the tiny kitten on the sofa and began to play
with him. 'I thought he was rather cute. Of course he'll
need somewhere to sleep, and you'll need some food
too——'

'*I* will?' Joanna walked around to face him, forgetting
her appearance for the moment, the fact that she looked
like an eighteen-year-old again, her hair soft, her face

163

completely free of make-up. 'Joshua, are you saying you're leaving this kitten *here*?' She watched as it skittered across the sofa, trying to attack Joshua's fingers.

He looked up at her. 'Don't you like him?' he repeated. 'I must say, it never occurred to me that you wouldn't want him.'

'I didn't say that,' she said irritably. 'I've just never had a cat before.'

'You had never had a dog either until you had Billy,' he shrugged. 'And look what a success that turned out to be.'

'But how did you get him?'

'Patrick bought him for Jonathan,' he mentioned Tina and Patrick's eldest son. 'And ever since they've had him in the house his nose has been streaming. Jonathan's, not the kitten's,' he added derisively.

'He's allergic to him?' she frowned.

'Right,' Joshua nodded. 'Of course I thought of you immediately they told me the problem. Billy was a birthday present for you, Sammy here was one for Jonathan. I didn't think you would like the idea of Sammy going back to the pet shop. He might not have been bought again,' he added pointedly.

Joanna doubted that this cute little bundle of fur and big eyes would ever have been passed over. He was about three months old, very cute, and he found the tassles on her curtains very interesting; he swung on them, his claws making tiny snags on the material.

'He needs a home, Joanna,' Joshua told her softly as she untangled the kitten from the curtains.

'Does he like milk?' She nuzzled her face into his soft fur.

'Loves it,' he nodded.

'What did you say this name was?'

'Sammy,' he drawled. 'Short for Samson.'

Her mouth quirked. 'Someone has a sense of humour.' The kitten couldn't have weighed more than a few ounces at most.

'Jonathan,' he nodded. 'Will you keep him or shall I try and find another home for him?'

'I'll keep him,' she smiled. 'I'll just take him through to the kitchen and get him some milk. Would you like some coffee?'

'Not for me, thanks.' He stood up, buttoning his coat. 'I started back at the clinic today in an advisory capacity. I'll see you later.' His lips claimed hers briefly. 'You and Sammy take care of each other until then.'

Joshua's surprise visit, his surprise gift, had started Joanna's day off right, and she talked softly to the kitten as he followed her about as she did her work, seeming to like her company as much as she welcomed his. She hadn't realised how alone she was, how much she needed someone or something to talk to, but it was amazing the warmth she felt when Sammy came to greet her as she came in from shopping for his food.

'I hear your husband is back.' James eyed her curiously later that afternoon as a gentle smile curved her lips.

She shot Dan an irritated glance, but he shrugged off the responsibility of telling the other man. 'That's right,' she confirmed softly.

'Do I take that to mean you'll be having a change of address in the near future?'

'No,' she smiled at his method of asking if she and Joshua were back together.

'No?' he frowned. 'Then the separation is permanent?'

'James, I don't think——'

'At the moment they're dating each other,' Dan put

in hastily, sensing she had been about to tell James to mind his own business.

'We aren't dating!' She turned her anger on Dan now. 'We're going out to dinner this evening, that's all. We've hardly had the opportunity to be alone, let alone talk to each other!'

'Last night was hardly my fault,' Dan snapped.

'No,' she accepted softly, knowing it had been her own lack of concentration that had made finishing the book such a rush at the end. 'I realise that. James, about the fifth book . . .'

'Yes?' The publisher was instantly on the alert.

'Could we delay it for a while? I need time to sort out my personal life.'

His mouth twisted. 'I seem to remember a self-possessed young lady telling me her marriage would have nothing to do with her career.'

Joanna blushed at the taunt. 'As my marriage stood then it wouldn't have done. Now it's a different matter completely.'

'And what about Dan?'

She chewed on her bottom lip, knowing that she had a responsibility to Dan, that he was contracted to do her illustrations, that he often turned down other work to do them.

'Don't worry about me,' he put in cheerfully. 'I happen to be going away for a while myself.'

'You do?' Two pairs of eyes focused on him in total surprise. A Londoner born and bred, Dan thought anywhere farther than Brighton was a foreign country.

'Carmella has a modelling contract in Japan for three months, she's asked me to go along for the trip,' he announced happily. 'I didn't think I'd be able to make it, but in the circumstances . . .'

'You're going to Japan?' Joanna asked incredulously.

'Why not?' He raised nonchalant brows.

'It's *thousands* of miles away!'

'So they tell me,' he nodded.

'But you hate travelling,' she reminded him dryly.

He grimaced. 'Not as much as I hate the idea of Carmella finding someone else while she's away.' He sighed. 'Who knows, I might do some work of my own while I'm over there.'

'You might.' Joanna was completely dazed. Dan must really be in love to consider leaving his beloved London for three months!

'Well, now that the two of you seem to have settled that matter between you,' James put in with brittle sarcasm, 'perhaps you wouldn't mind telling me how I explain the delay to the public?'

'You haven't even published this fourth book yet,' Joanna reasoned.

'Nevertheless, the fifth one is scheduled to be on my desk, completed, in six months' time.'

'You'll have it,' she promised.

James frowned. 'You'll write it in three months?'

'In three *weeks* if I have to,' she nodded.

'All right,' he shrugged. 'Make the arrangements between the two of you.'

'He just wants the book on his desk in six months,' Dan muttered as they left the building.

'He has a point, Dan,' Joanna sighed. 'We left it a bit short notice to tell him we're both taking three months off.'

'I suppose so,' he nodded. 'Like to come and have a coffee with me somewhere?'

She shook her head. 'I have to get back and feed Sammy.'

'Sammy?'

She explained about the kitten. 'He's really sweet,'

she smiled. 'He almost looked sad to see me go when I left earlier.'

The kitten was fast asleep on her bed when she got home, although he had knocked her box of tissues on the floor and ripped them to shreds before he went to sleep. With an indulgent smile at the gently breathing creature Joanna picked the shredded tissue up off the floor. Who knew, in a few months' time she might have enough material for a mischievous cat story!

When the doorbell rang a few minutes later she knew it was Joshua; she sensed it even before she opened the door. Her smile deepened as she saw it was indeed him. 'Why didn't you use your key?' she asked as they went into the lounge. 'It would save you the trouble of waiting for me to answer the door.'

'It would also be an invasion of your privacy,' he drawled. 'I just thought I would check how the kitten is?'

'Asleep,' she still smiled.

'Has he settled down okay? He's no trouble to you?' he frowned.

'None at all. I love him already. Have you come to cancel dinner?' she asked anxiously.

'No,' he smiled. 'I left the clinic early; I don't officially take over again until next month. I thought I would just check on you and Sammy before I went home.'

Home. Once again she wondered where that was for him at the moment. But she didn't feel confident enough with him to dare ask again. 'As you can see, we're both fine,' she laughed as Sammy bounced out of her bedroom and ran straight up the curtains.

'I don't think the same can be said for your curtains,' Joshua said dryly as he 'rescued' the balancing kitten from the curtain rail. 'Here,' he handed the unrepentant Sammy to her. 'You have a nice home,' he frowned. 'I'd hate to think a kitten I gave you was going to ruin it for you.'

'I don't mind in the least,' she assured him, absently stroking the kitten. 'Billy was much worse than this.'

'So I gathered,' he nodded. 'Well, now that I've ascertained that you're both all right I'll be on my way.'

'Joshua——'

'Yes?' He looked at her with narrowed eyes.

'Do you—Is there a telephone number where I can reach you?' asked Joanna in a rush before she lost her nerve. 'In case anything like last night ever happens again. Not that I expect it to, in fact I'm taking a short break from writing now that I have that book out of the way. I just wouldn't like you to be inconvenienced again.'

Joshua buttoned his coat ready to face the icy February weather outside. 'It wasn't an inconvenience,' he dismissed abruptly, making no effort to give her a telephone number.

Of course he wouldn't want her telephoning him, she berated herself once he had left. What would Angela think—or say—if she should answer the call! How ironic that, for the moment—she refused to think it was permanent!—the wife should be the 'other woman'.

But it wouldn't remain that way, she was determined on that! Joshua was her husband, and although she hadn't been willing to fight for him a year ago, she was desperate for him now.

She dressed with special care in the red dress later that evening, the height of her sandals giving her a look of elegance, every slender curve of her body flattered by the style of the dress, her make-up light and glowing, her hair soft and silky.

It was the latter Joshua complimented her on. 'I always preferred your hair longer,' he turned to smile at her as they sat side by side in the Rolls, Joshua driving them himself. 'The way it was when I first met you. You looked a little like Alice in Wonderland then.'

'I was a brat,' she said abruptly.

He laughed at the disgust in her voice. 'No, you weren't. A little wilful, perhaps, but never a brat.'

'Oh yes,' she nodded, 'I was. I saw something I wanted, and regardless of whether or not I was wanted in return, I was determined to have you.'

'I didn't put up much of a fight,' he derided.

'But you did!' She turned in her seat to look at him. 'You didn't want to have anything to do with me, and you were so good about my pestering you too. I'm surprised you didn't put me over your knee and spank me,' she added ruefully.

'I thought about it,' he admitted. 'But it wouldn't have done any good, I would only have ended up making love to you afterwards.'

'You would?' Her eyes widened.

Joshua glanced at her with raised brows. 'Did you doubt it?'

'But I forced the situation on you, I forced *myself* on you,' she persisted.

'A man of thirty-two doesn't let a girl of seventeen *force* herself on him. I wanted you too, Joanna, I thought you realised that,' he frowned.

She moistened her lips, surprise and puzzlement reflected in the blue depths of her eyes. 'You thought I was older, I lied about my age——'

'And I knew you were nowhere near being the twenty you claimed to be. Admittedly seventeen was a little lower than my estimation, I would have said at least eighteen, but I certainly knew you weren't twenty. I wanted you, anyway.'

'I never knew that,' she said breathlessly.

Joshua shrugged. 'We've never spoken of it before, so how could you?' he dismissed.

Joanna realised now that they had never really spoken about anything of importance in the whole of the five years they had been together, that she had come to know him better the last few days than in the years of their marriage.

'Oh, before I forget,' he put his hand into his jacket pocket, taking something out to hand it to her. 'It belongs to Sammy. I picked it up from Patrick's.'

She took the small toy mouse, not even realising she had put it in her evening bag. 'This morning?' she frowned.

'No, this evening,' he told her curtly.

'But——'

'I'm staying with Tina and Patrick at the moment, Joanna,' he said abruptly.

'Tina and——! But I thought——'

'Yes?' he prompted tautly.

'Angela . . .?'

He seemed to stiffen. 'What about her?'

'You aren't staying with her?' She was tense as she waited for his answer.

'I just told you, I'm staying with Tina and Patrick,' he repeated patiently.

'But if you aren't staying with Angela why aren't you staying with me?' She drew in a ragged breath as she realised how demanding she sounded. 'I mean, I have plenty of room. It would have been no trouble——'

'It wouldn't have worked out, Joanna,' he sighed.

It wouldn't have worked out. Why wouldn't it?—she wanted to scream. But she already had her answer. Joshua didn't want to live with her any more, and he had been trying to let her down gently.

'Where is Angela?' she asked dully.

'Still in the States. She married a doctor out there two months ago.'

So she wasn't even fighting a mistress any more, she was just fighting the fact that Joshua didn't love her, that he had never loved her. Even the kitten had probably been a way of softening the blow, of giving her something of her own to love after he had gone. As if a kitten, no matter how cute and loving, could ever make up for losing the man she loved!

All the enjoyment in the evening had gone for her, and she just wanted to get home and lick her wounds in private. But she saw the evening through, even managed to make light conversation, although she saw Joshua shoot her several probing glances as their meal progressed.

What was she supposed to do, break down in front of him and cry? Maybe she would have done if she hadn't known that all she would get from him would be pity. And she didn't want his pity, she had known his passion, his compassion, his sympathy, his coldness— pity was the last thing she could accept from him now.

'Would you mind if we called it a night?' she said once he had driven her home, her nerves stretched to breaking point. 'I had a busy day yesterday, and I–I feel tired tonight.'

'Of course.' He switched off the gentle purr of the engine and turned to take her into his arms.

'It really is very late,' she evaded his touch. 'Sammy will want feeding, and he's very young to be left on his own for so long.'

'Joanna?' Joshua frowned his puzzlement in the gloom of the car.

She managed a light laugh. 'I'm just tired.'

'If you're sure that's all it is. The lobster——'

'Was delicious,' she assured him. 'Don't worry, I'm

not going to embarrass you by being sick like I was the last time I ate it.'

'You didn't embarrass me,' he rasped. 'And that particular restaurant thought twice before serving lobster to one of its customers again,' he added grimly.

Her eyes widened. 'You complained?'

'I did more than that,' he bit out. 'I threatened them with a health inspector. You could have died!'

'I was a little sick, but——'

'You were very ill,' he corrected harshly. 'I wouldn'+ want to sit through three nights like that again.'

'No,' she turned away. 'Well, it isn't tha+ this evening, it's just tiredness.' She opened the door and got out of the car. 'Thank you for tonight, Joshua, I had—Oh!' Suddenly he was standing next to her on the pavement. She looked up at him unflinchingly. 'I had a lovely time.'

'Did you?' His dark frown was clearly discernible in the lamplight.

'Very nice,' she nodded, turning her face away as he would have kissed her.

Puzzlement flickered in stormy grey eyes. 'Joanna?'

'Not here in the street, Joshua.' Her head was thrown back proudly.

'Then let's go into your flat.' He grasped her arm.

'Not tonight, Joshua,' her voice was sharp in her tension, 'I'm really not—not in the mood.'

'I see.' His hand dropped away from her arm. 'Can I see you tomorrow?'

'I—I'm not sure.' She made a show of searching in her bag for her door key. 'Mother said something about dinner . . .' she told him vaguely.

'Maybe I could come too?'

Stupid, stupid, *stupid*! Her parents were the last people she should have used as an excuse for not seeing him tomorrow; he knew exactly how welcome he always was with them. 'I—er—I'm sure you can. Why don't you ring me tomorrow and I can let you know the arrangements?' she said brightly.

'I'll ring you in the afternoon,' he nodded abruptly. 'You're sure you feel all right?'

'I feel fine,' she told him lightly. 'I'll see you tomorrow.'

'Joanna!' His sharp command forced her to stop, and she turned slowly to face him. 'Don't husbands get a goodnight kiss any more?'

She raised up on tiptoe and kissed him on the cheek, moving away as he would have turned his mouth to hers. 'Thank you once again for tonight, Joshua,' she said with cool politeness, leaving him without hindrance this time.

Once she was in bed she cried as she hadn't cried for months, soaking poor Sammy's fur as he tried to comfort her. During the early hours of the morning, as sleep still eluded her, she came to a decision. At the moment Joshua felt responsible for her, felt compelled to see her, to try and explain that she no longer had a part in his life, her own obvious change of heart about their marriage making this difficult for him. As from tomorrow he wouldn't need to feel responsible for her any more, because she didn't intend being here.

Dan's flat was much more stark than her own, his tastes obviously more masculine and not exactly homely. But she appreciated him letting her use the flat while he and Carmella were in France for the weekend on a modelling assignment.

'She's weaning me away from London gradually,' he explained ruefully when Joanna turned up on his doorstep with a case in one hand and Sammy in the other. 'We go to Japan next week. I never thought I would end up trailing around the world after any woman,' he added derisively.

He continued to talk, and Joanna knew it was for her sake, because he sensed her complete desolation. She had arrived fifteen minutes earlier, bursting into tears as she threw herself into his arms, although he didn't probe her deep hurt as she seemed numb after her tears had ceased. And he still hadn't probed, accepting that she had been hurt badly and needed a refuge.

'He's a cute little chap.' He was tickling Sammy's tummy. 'Joshua gave him to you, you said?'

'That's right,' she nodded. 'He's his replacement,' she added with bitterness.

'Jo——'

'Forget I said that,' she dismissed harshly. 'You're sure you don't mind the two of us staying here for a few days?' she determinedly talked about something else.

'Be my guest,' he shrugged. 'But if you're intending hiding out from Joshua here I don't think you'll be successful. We work together, this is one of the first places he'll look. This is almost as bad as your own flat.'

'Except that he still has a key to that,' she reminded him. 'Here I don't have to answer the door or telephone if I don't want to.'

'He could break the door down,' Dan warned.

'He doesn't want to see me that badly,' Joanna said dryly. 'As long as he thinks there's no one here he'll go away.'

'Okay,' Dan shrugged. 'You know him better than I do. I'll move in with Carmella until we go to France tomorrow. That way I won't have to answer the door and let you down. I'm a terrible liar, Jo.'

Did Dan really think she knew Joshua better than he

did? God, she didn't know her husband at all!

When the knock sounded on Dan's door later that night she knew it was Joshua, knew it even before he began to call Dan's name. When he still received no answer he began to talk to her. 'I know you're in there, Joanna,' he told her angrily. 'Now open this door and talk to me! Damn it, don't you owe me some sort of explanation? Joanna, open this door!' His voice rose in volume, and a few seconds later a door could be heard opening, voices raised angrily as one of the other tenants demanded to know what was going on. Then a door slammed shut. 'I'll check around some more, Joanna,' Joshua's voice was softer this time, but no less threatening. 'And if I can't find you I'll know for certain you're here, and I'll be back. I'll be back, Joanna!'

She shivered with reaction once he had gone, hardly daring to move in case he hadn't actually left but was still waiting outside. How long she sat there she didn't know, but finally it was Sammy who woke her out of her daze, jumping on to her lap and purring loudly.

For the next two days no one came to the door, although she couldn't relax, couldn't sleep; there were dark circles beneath her eyes, her hair was dull and lifeless, all food tasting like cardboard to her.

This was so much worse than anything she had ever felt before, even worse than when Lindy died. Then she had simply withdrawn, become cold and aloof, now she was having to suffer the loss of Joshua all in one terrible nightmare, and the pain was almost more than she could bear.

She was in the kitchen making herself a cup of tea when on the third day she heard a key in the lock and the sound of voices. Dan was back!

She rushed out of the kitchen, very pale and drawn in

a navy blue jumper and tight denims, her hair secured at her nape with a blue ribbon. Her hand shook badly as she saw Joshua entering the flat with Dan, and the latter hurried to take the cup out of her hand before she spilt the scalding liquid over herself.

'Jo——'

'Could you leave us alone, please, Dan?' Joshua rasped, his gaze fixed on Joanna. 'Joanna and I have some talking to do—in private.'

'No!' She clutched on to Dan's arm. 'Don't leave me,' she pleaded with him. 'Please, don't leave me!'

Icy grey eyes narrowed on her; Joshua was pale and haggard himself. 'You really want a witness to our conversation?' he bit out tautly.

Joanna swallowed hard. 'I don't want there to be a conversation. I already know what you're going to say, and you can have your divorce. I won't fight it or make a scene.'

'Divorce?' He seemed to pale even more. 'I don't want a divorce!'

'Of course you do,' she scorned.

'No——'

'I'll be in the bedroom,' Dan cut in hastily. 'This conversation really is too private. I'll be here if you need me, Jo,' he squeezed her hand reassuringly, glancing over at the rigid-jawed Joshua, 'but I don't think you will.'

'Dan——'

'Let him go,' Joshua rasped as she would have stopped the other man, the bedroom door closing softly a few seconds later. 'Now why should you think I want a divorce?' he demanded to know.

'Isn't it obvious?'

'Not to me!'

'I don't need your pity——'

'Pity?' he echoed forcefully, striding over to grasp her shoulders and shake her roughly. 'When have I ever shown you pity?'

'Taking me out, giving me the kitten. It would have been kinder just to come straight out and tell me you want a divorce.' She pulled away from him, clasping her hands together to stop them shaking. 'You didn't have to go through this charade of taking me out first. I'm no longer a child——'

'I do not want a divorce!'

She turned to look at him, frowning her bewilderment. He sounded so sincere, almost angry at the suggestion, and yet he must want a divorce, why else would he say living at her flat with her wouldn't have worked out?

'Joanna?' he frowned at her silence.

'I can take it, Joshua,' she told him shakily. 'As I said, I'm no longer a child.'

'You're acting like one!'

She flushed. 'On the contrary, I'm being very adult. I'm giving you what you want without any fuss.'

'What I want?' he echoed in a deceptively soft voice. *'What I want?'* he thundered this time. 'What I want is you back, as my wife, in my home, in my bed. *That's* what I want!'

'But—I——'

'It obviously isn't going to work out that way,' he rasped coldly. 'I should have realised the night I got back and found you surrounded by all your friends. You don't need me, you don't need anyone. But I tried—I tried to give you what I thought you needed,' he said bleakly.

'Wh-what did I need, Joshua?' she questioned, still not too sure why he should say he wanted her back *now*. If it were still only pity—then she didn't want to know!

'When we met, when I got you pregnant, you were barely more than a child yourself. I'd deprived you of all the friendships and boy-friends you should have had during those early years——'

'No——'

'Oh yes,' he insisted grimly. 'And you were obviously enjoying your freedom when I got back, showed no sign of wanting to move back to the house with me.' He drew in a ragged breath. 'At first I thought of staying on at the flat, of making you want me, of seducing you back into the marriage that way. But after only one night I realised I couldn't do that to you again. I decided to—to move out and court you.'

Joanna's eyes widened. '*Court* me?'

'Yes,' he hissed. 'You're my wife, but you never had a courtship from me, not from anyone really. Maybe that's why you've had no idea what the last few days have been about, the dinners together, the kisses goodnight but no further—and God knows I wanted to go further!' he rasped grimly. 'The kitten was a gift to you from me—Jonathan had nothing to do with it. Billy had meant so much to you, I wanted to be the one to help ease the loss you still seemed to feel for him, a certain sadness that comes through in your books. But another dog was out of the question, you said yourself that Billy couldn't be replaced that way. So I bought you the kitten and kept him at Patrick's that morning before I brought him over to you; Jonathan would have kept him if I'd let him.'

'But you told me——'

He sighed. 'I wasn't sure you would accept such a gift from me. But I thought if you came to love Sammy perhaps you would come to love me too.' He grimaced. 'Instead of which you've now asked me for a divorce.'

She shook her head dazedly. 'No——'

'I won't stand in your way, Joanna.' He grasped her arms, his gaze intent on her pale face. 'That was the deal we made when we agreed to separate for a year. I'll give you your freedom.'

'But——'

'Just let me hold you, kiss you once more!' he groaned, his mouth moving druggingly over hers, holding her against him as if he would never let her go. 'I love you, Joanna,' he told her gruffly when he at last raised his head. 'I'll always love you.'

Before she could answer him, before she could tell him she loved him in return, he had released her and strode out of the flat.

CHAPTER TEN

'WELL, you aren't just going to stand there, are you?' drawled a taunting voice. 'I hope you're going after him.'

Joanna turned to find Dan had left his bedroom and was now looking at her challengingly. 'You heard?'

'Most of it,' he nodded, coming further into the room. 'The walls on this flat aren't very thick. Knowing you were pregnant when you got married answers a lot of things that have been puzzling me.'

'Namely why Joshua married me in the first place,' she said dryly.

'No, I already knew that he loved you,' Dan chided. 'Do you have any idea how we came to arrive here together today?'

She was so dazed by having Joshua tell her he loved her that how he came to be here didn't seem important. He *loved* her—she could hardly believe that. Love had never been mentioned in their relationship in the past, not even at the height of their physical pleasure in each other. Could it be that they had both been frightened to say the actual words?

'Because I'm going to tell you,' Dan said firmly. 'He came to France. Yes,' he nodded at the surprised widening of her eyes, 'he found the agency Carmella works for, found out where we were, and came out there. You wouldn't even acknowledge that you were here, let alone see him; the man had no choice. I told him it would have been easier to break the door down,' he mocked his own fear of three days ago. 'But he said he didn't want to frighten you, that you had already suffered enough in your marriage. He loves you so much, Jo. He was out of his mind with worry until I told him you were definitely here. Now if you don't go after him you aren't the woman I thought you were.'

She swallowed hard, bewildered as to the lengths Joshua had gone just to speak to her. He must love her, there could be no other explanation. 'Where do you think he's gone, Dan?' She was pulling on her coat with hurried movements.

He shrugged. 'Where did he go in the past when he had to get away from you?'

'His mistress,' she said tightly.

Dan sighed. 'He won't have gone to see her this time,' he chided.

'The clinic, then,' she frowned. 'Do you really think I drove him away from me in the past, Dan?'

'Only you can answer that, love.'

And she knew the answer only too well. She had forced Joshua into taking a mistress, had given him no other choice. Had he loved her even then, as Dan said he did? She had to know, had to tell him that she had loved him from the first.

The woman behind the reception desk at Joshua's private practice was new to her, a replacement Patrick had found for Angela a year ago. She raised blonde brows in astonishment when Joanna introduced herself.

'Is my husband here?' she wanted to know.

'Well, yes. But——'

'In his surgery?'

'Yes, but——'

'Then perhaps you could see that we aren't disturbed?' she requested politely.

'But, Mrs Radcliffe——'

'Yes?' She paused at the door.

'Mr Radcliffe said he was unavailable to everyone.'

'That doesn't include me,' she told the woman haughtily, knowing that she hardly looked the part of Joshua's wife in her navy blue jumper and the tight denims, her hair still secured by the ribbon at her nape. 'Don't worry,' she smiled. 'He'll want to see me.' She spoke with much more confidence than she felt, although it seemed to have convinced the receptionist, for the other woman subsided into her chair with a rueful shrug.

Joanna knew elation that Joshua was at least here, but nervousness for the next few minutes. They would be the deciding point for the rest of her life.

Joshua lay back in the chair behind his desk, his eyes closed, his face pale. His lids flickered open as he heard her softly close the door, seeming to swallow convulsively as he stiffened.

She moved to stand in front of the desk. 'I don't want a divorce, Joshua,' she spoke slowly, clearly. 'I didn't want to be parted from you for the last year either. That last night we were together, I tried to tell you I loved you—I hadn't even realised I still did until then. But I——'

'Still?' he repeated that word almost dazedly.

'I loved you in Canada, Joshua,' she explained gently. 'I loved you all the time we were married, but when Lindy died——'

'You blamed me,' he said heavily, deep lines of harshness grooved into his face.

'No!' she frowned. 'Of course not. Why should you think that?'

'I was a doctor——'

'But you couldn't perform miracles, Joshua. If anyone was to blame it was me.'

'You?' he gasped. 'No one could have loved her more than you did!'

'But I wanted to kill her before she was even born, remember,' she said bitterly.

His expression softened. 'Not really. You were just a frightened child. It didn't take much to persuade you that it wasn't the answer.' He stood up to come to her, stopping several inches away from actual contact. 'Have you been blaming yourself all this time?'

'Have you?'

'God!' he breathed raggedly.

'At first, after she died,' she had to talk now, to tell him everything, she might never have the courage to do so again!—'I couldn't bear you to make love to me because I thought that every time you touched me you would blame me for Lindy's death. Then after a while it became simpler, easier, to just believe I hated you, you and the marriage I was trapped in.'

'You did hate me,' he said heavily. 'How could you not when I tried to make love to you the day after Lindy died?'

'I understand that now, Joshua.' She met his gaze steadily. 'I would have understood it then if I hadn't been so concerned with my own guilt and grief.' She sighed deeply. 'The only time we were ever close, ever really communicated, was when we made love. That was it, wasn't it, Joshua, you wanted to be close to me in the only way you knew how?' She had realised a lot of things on the drive over here, and Joshua's need to make love to her that night was one of them.

'Yes,' he acknowledged tautly. 'But I could see you hated me after that, and rather than face the problem and risk losing you, I started staying out of the house. It didn't seem to bother you when I went to work in the evenings, you just carried on with your life as if I didn't exist.'

'I forced you to turn to Angela, I know that——'

'But I didn't,' he shook his head. 'I haven't touched another woman since we were in Canada together.'

'But you said——'

'I told you I'd slept with Angela for six months, and I had, two years before I ever met you.'

Joanna gasped. 'Then this time in America——'

'Spent working, nothing else.'

'And you let me think you were going away with her, that you would be sleeping with her. You told me to take a lover—*lovers*!' she reminded him indignantly.

'And it nearly killed me,' he rasped. 'When I first got back I thought Dan was your lover; I could have ripped him apart limb from limb! At the party—'

'The party was for you, for your homecoming,' she told him quickly. 'But you didn't come home, and the invitations had already gone out.'

'I didn't realise that,' he shook his head. 'I just thought you and Dan were giving the party, and he certainly went out of his way that night to give the impression that you were more than friends. When he didn't stay the night I thought perhaps I'd been wrong after all, that he'd just been protecting you. He was, wasn't he?'

'Yes,' she nodded. 'Joshua—that last night, couldn't you *tell* I loved you?'

'I could tell you wanted me to *make* love to you. But I'd promised you a year, I owed you that much.'

'But I didn't want it,' she told him desperately. 'That night I came out of the cold daze I'd been in since Lindy died, I was even planning to come to the States with you. But in the morning you'd gone, to be with Angela, I thought.'

Joshua shook his head. 'I didn't want any other woman after you, Joanna. In Canada, when I first started to notice you, I thought you were an attractive little minx. Then I realised you were getting under my skin, that I was even beginning to look out for you as the days passed. But I made no effort to get to know you better, I knew you were too young for me, that I should never have become involved with you. But I couldn't resist you, and when you came to my cabin——'

'I forced the situation.'

'How many times do I have to tell you I wasn't forced?' he bit out angrily. 'I fell in love with you that night.'

'How could you have done?' she gasped incredulously. 'You didn't even come and say goodbye to me the next morning.'

'Because I didn't realise you were leaving that early! I slept late,' his mouth twisted self-derisively. 'Then I went out and had some breakfast. By the time I got to your cabin you'd already left. The manager of the cabins was of the opinion that you'd returned to England. I left the next day as planned, and when I tried calling your home I was told you were in Florida.' His expression was grim.

'You called my home?' Her eyes were wide.

'Yes,' he confirmed woodenly. 'You'd gone off on another holiday, when you would probably take more lovers, I thought.'

'I went with my parents straight from Canada. And it was the most miserable time of my life. You see, I came to your cabin that last morning, and when you weren't there I thought you'd gone skiing as you usually did, that I'd meant nothing to you. I had no idea you had gone into town to get some breakfast. I just thought I'd been a holiday affair to you, like Mari was.'

'No.' His jaw tightened. 'But I had the feeling that's all I'd been to you.'

'Was that the reason you thought I was pregnant by someone else?' she frowned. 'Because you thought I'd used you as my *first* sexual experiment?'

'Yes,' he sighed. 'But then I realised you would hardly have come to me if it were another man's child. Do you know what it did to me to know you only came to see me because you were expecting my child? When I saw your appointment in the book I had such high hopes, and when I knew the truth . . . God, it was hell! You felt so trapped—'

'So did you!'

'Not really. Admittedly it wasn't the way I would have planned to marry you, but it did make you my wife. And for a while we were like any other married couple, living together, laughing together, buying things for the baby we were expecting. But when Lindy was born and we knew how ill she was you became distant from me—mentally, not physically. As the months, years passed, I just became grateful for the fact that you were my wife. When we were first married I'd given you a bedroom of your own so that you wouldn't feel trapped into a physical relationship with me. There were nights after Lindy died that I was glad of that, nights when I almost went out of my mind thinking about you. If you'd been in the same bed as me every night I would have gone insane!'

'I never knew, never realised . . .'

'That I love you, that I've always loved you?' Joshua sighed raggedly. 'I didn't want you to know. I didn't want your pity.'

'But I've always loved you too. I tried to show you, when you came back from the States, that I wanted us to start again. I cleared Lindy's room of all memories in an effort to show you I was ready to start afresh.'

'And I thought you'd done it because you were ready

to put our marriage and everything about it behind you.' He heaved a deep sigh of regret. 'How can two relatively intelligent people——'

'Brilliant in your case, darling,' Joanna murmured, moving into his arms, caressing his face with shaking fingertips.

'How can we have been so damned stupid?' he groaned.

'Lack of communication,' she shrugged dismissal of those troubled years. 'But it won't happen again. I intend telling you my every thought in future. I hope you'll do the same?' She looked up at him anxiously.

'Oh, I'll do the same,' he said throatily. 'For instance, right now I'm thinking——' he bent lower and whispered the rest of his thoughts in her ear.

A slow smile spread over her face. 'Strange, I was thinking the same thing,' she glowed up at him. 'And I always thought one of these lovely couches in your consulting-room would be a perfect place to make love.'

'Here?' His eyes widened.

'Why not?' she teased.

'Why not, indeed?' he agreed throatily. 'God, I love you, Joanna,' he added raggedly.

'Just keep telling me that!' She melted against him.

'Oh, I will!' he gave her a lifelong promise.

Harlequin Plus
DELIGHTFUL DELECTABLE RIBS

You don't have to be a gourmet cook, or spend hours haunting specialty-food shops searching for ingredients your grocery store doesn't carry, to produce tasty dishes your family and friends will love. One meat that is easy to prepare and is always a favorite is pork spareribs—just ask Joshua, Carole Mortimer's hero! Following is perhaps the world's simplest sparerib recipe. The cooking time is long, but don't be daunted. You needn't spend all the time in the kitchen. While the ribs are cooking, you may prepare other items for the table, or watch television, or read a Harlequin!

What you need:

2 lbs. back spareribs
2 tbsp. vegetable oil
1 can tomato soup, undiluted
1 cup water

2 medium onions, peeled and halved
1 tsp. Worchestershire sauce
freshly ground pepper

What to do:

Cut ribs into serving-size pieces (two or three ribs each) and brown on high heat in oil in large heavy skillet. Remove ribs and set aside. Turn heat to medium and add soup, water, onion, Worchestershire sauce and pepper. Stir. Return ribs to skillet. Cover and simmer $1^{1}/_{2}$ - 2 hours, turning occasionally and adding a little water if sauce becomes too thick. Ribs are done when meat is so tender it almost falls off the bones. Place ribs on a serving platter, pour sauce over them and serve. Delicious!

Take these
4 best-selling novels
FREE

as advertised on **TV**

Yes! Four sophisticated,
contemporary love stories
by four world-famous
authors of romance
FREE, as your
introduction to the Harlequin Presents
subscription plan. Thrill to **Anne Mather**'s
passionate story BORN OUT OF LOVE, set
in the Caribbean.... Travel to darkest Africa
in **Violet Winspear**'s TIME OF THE TEMPTRESS....Let
Charlotte Lamb take you to the fascinating world of London's
Fleet Street in MAN'S WORLD.... Discover beautiful Greece in
Sally Wentworth's moving romance SAY HELLO TO YESTERDAY

Harlequin Presents...

*The very finest
in romance fiction*

Join the millions of avid Harlequin readers all over the
world who delight in the magic of a really exciting novel.
EIGHT great NEW titles published EACH MONTH!
Each month you will get to know exciting, interesting,
true-to-life people .... You'll be swept to distant lands you've
dreamed of visiting .... Intrigue, adventure, romance, and
the destiny of many lives will thrill you through each
Harlequin Presents novel.

Get all the latest books before they're sold out!
As a Harlequin subscriber you actually receive your
personal copies of the latest Presents novels immediately
after they come off the press, so you're sure of getting all
8 each month.

Cancel your subscription whenever you wish!
You don't have to buy any minimum number of books.
Whenever you decide to stop your subscription just let us
know and we'll cancel all further shipments.

Harlequin reaches
into the hearts and minds
of women across America
to bring you

Harlequin American Romance ™·

YOURS FREE!

Get this book FREE!

Mail to:
Harlequin Reader Service

In the U.S.
2504 West Southern Avenue
Tempe, AZ 85282

In Canada
649 Ontario Street
Stratford, Ontario N5A 6W2

YES! I want to be one of the first to discover **Harlequin American Romance.** Send me FREE and without obligation *Twice in a Lifetime*. If you do not hear from me after I have examined my FREE book, please send me the 4 new **Harlequin American Romances** each month as soon as they come off the presses. I understand that I will be billed only $2.25 for each book (total $9.00). There are no shipping or handling charges. There is no minimum number of books that I have to purchase. In fact, I may cancel this arrangement at any time. *Twice in a Lifetime* is mine to keep as a FREE gift, even if I do not buy any additional books. 154 BPA NARV

Name _____ (please print)

Address _____ Apt. no.

City _____ State/Prov. _____ Zip/Postal Code

Signature (If under 18, parent or guardian must sign.)